# THE RIVER OF DREAMS

## A COLLECTION OF STORIES

BY

GLENN NAYLOR

*This book is dedicated to my wife, Jan.*

GLENN NAYLOR



First published in Great Britain in 2022 by Riverhead



A CIP catalogue record for this book is available from the British Library

ISBN 978-1-9164294-6-8

Design and Production by Riverhead, Hull
Telephone: 07890 170063
email: mike.riverheadbooks@gmail.com

Printed by: Fisk Printers, Hull

ACKNOWLEDGEMENT
I'd like to sincerely thank Mike Sterriker at Riverhead for his help and advice in writing and publishing this book.

FRONT COVER PHOTOGRAPH:
'Sunlight on the Humber' by Jane Sturdy

# CONTENTS

Prince Street in Hull's Old Town

# GLAD ALL OVER

He was walking towards me, staggering almost.

Still smartly dressed: usual collar and tie and long navy blue overcoat. Hair greyer now, features of a hardened drinker. But it was him all right: ex Detective Chief Inspector Barry Donegal.

By the looks of him, no longer Sweeney Todd's finest: Sweeney Todd - Flying Squad, as it was known back in the day.

I'd returned to Hull, UK City of Culture, to drop in on my younger brother, who'd waxed lyrical about the forthcoming events of early 2017 for quite some time. He clearly wanted me to see his contribution: an oil painting in the local art gallery.

Couldn't imagine Donegal being a culture vulture. Good detective he may have been, but he was as rough as... And that's being complimentary!

We passed each other. Not sure he recognised me. Nor was I sure I wanted to be. But I was curious.

He had no family ties left in Hull. Turned my head, saw him tentatively threading his way through the barricaded footpath renovations.

Followed him at a discreet distance for several minutes before he obeyed the 'little green man' and crossed over the road to the transport interchange: train or bus?

Neither.

Made his way into The Royal Hotel.

Checked my watch: eleven-thirty am. Late morning

snifter: no change there.

Donegal positioned himself at the far end of the bar, arms resting atop. I took hold of a newspaper from the reception desk, taking in the splendid Victorian architecture, the ceiling in particular. Never ceased to amaze me.

Located myself as far away from my old DCI as possible, without losing sight of him.

He only sipped his lager at first, then, with a couple of generous gulps, it was gone. Seemed nervous, looking around from time to time, causing me at one juncture to swiftly hide my face with the Guardian.

Not content with the lager, he ordered a large Scotch, which he studied before pulling out his smart-phone: seemed to be sending a text.

Not long before his phone emitted that somewhat irritating tone signifying a reply. Donegal checked it, downed his Scotch in one and purposefully strode towards the front exit.

It was bitingly cold outside, then again, it was January. Not only did I require my flat cap to deflect the chill, I didn't want Donegal to identify me. Yet.

His next port of call was the strangely named public house Hull Cheese. Brought my newspaper with me and appropriately seated myself. Donegal showed he'd lost none of his fondness for a double malt.

Piped music - for the enjoyment of the clientele no doubt: some soppy ballad from The Eighties replaced with the raucous, but muted rendition of The Dave Clark Five singing 'Glad All Over'.

Visibly uplifted, Donegal was tapping his fingers on the bar in time with the chorus.

*I'm feelin' glad all over*
*Yes I'm glad all over*
*Baby I'm glad all over*
*So glad you're mine*

It was his song, even more so when we became detectives in the Met, celebrating closure of a case. But it was mid 1980s when we established ourselves as a team, me a uniformed constable, Donegal a sergeant in blue. Drafted onto the miners' picket lines to cope with the strike, both of us helping to resist the stubborn resistance of Kent pitmen at Tilmanstone Colliery. In Donegal's case it was more than resistance: positively gung-ho.

One incident involved him chasing a young miner, who'd broken away from the lines, rugby tackling him and kicking him in the ribs as he lay on the ground.

I couldn't let this go: pulled my sergeant off the youngster, resulting in Donegal shouting at me, "See these stripes, Constable? As your superior officer they give me the right to do what I am going to do now."

He clattered me on the side of my face with a right hander, which dislodged my helmet. Unfortunately for me, Inspector Rossington witnessed this unseemly skirmish and proceeded to deliver a right condescending bollicking, "Don't prevent Sergeant Donegal from honing his skills required for the Flying Squad. There's a good lad."

Flying Squad? First I'd heard.

Couple of years later: I'm a Detective Sergeant with Detective Inspector Donegal.

In the Flying Squad he was successful. Lost count of the number of times "Glad All Over" reverberated through New Scotland Yard's corridors.

Possibly his crowning glory was November 1990: attempted armed robbery on a Securicor vehicle containing around three-quarter of a million pounds.

Operation Yamoto, that was it. Even though we'd had good intelligence I remember Donegal being unusually nervous on this operation.

He was right to be so: shooters were involved. Any hits from our marksmen and the Police Complaints Authority move in.

Not saying anything was amiss on Yamoto. But Donegal wasn't a 'by the book' detective. Consequently, The PCA, for him, were persone non grata. Sure enough, one of the armed robbers was shot dead, another wounded in the shoulder. However, apart from some inter-departmental wrangling between the Met and Surrey, all was fine: feelin' glad all over.

That was then.

Now, he's a... well, I'm not one for clichés normally... but, a shadow of his former self is an understatement.

Engaged in chit-chat with the barman, I moved over to the bar myself, making a show of reading my newspaper. Glad I didn't have to read it for real; Trump and Brexit dominate.

When the barman asked if I'd like a drink, Donegal turned his head towards me when I mumbled 'Jack Daniels'.

Don't think he clocked me, not with my recent facial acquisition and a gap of sixteen years. But out of my eye corner: Donegal's memory bank revolving like a tic-tac-toe machine. Been rumbled?

Some detective!

Donegal's phone burst into life: half expected a Glad All Over ringtone. Instead it was worse: Theme from Superman.

A suppressed laugh became a snigger, which I guess, fortunately for me, was drowned out by the snatch of music.

This was a thankful diversion: the ex DCI spoke in a low voice.

The word Minerva alerted me. The Minerva is a

public house near the old pier in Hull's Old Town overlooking a brown, swirling mass of water: the River Humber. Took a chance on Donegal's next port of call being this rather quaint drinking establishment, casually folding my paper, which I tucked under arm after downing my bourbon in one.

The wind sweeping off the Humber penetrated my thinly layered clothing: fashion is all very well, but...

Late afternoon, but, unusually, for a pub these days, well populated. Senior Citizens prominent, probably taking advantage of the reasonably priced food. Not a lager lout in sight.

The Minerva had retained the original layout, with inviting nooks and snugs. If Donegal was on his way, where would he position himself; he'd already, possibly, identified me.

Concealing myself wouldn't be easy; wanted to be close enough to sus what he was up to. Decided to exit. And wait.

Far enough away not to be seen, nearer enough, hopefully, to see Donegal enter the premises. Fifteen shivering minutes later that familiar navy-blue overcoat wafted around a corner, it's owner scanning the locality for... someone like me. Once a detective...

Wondered if I could discern anything looking through a window. Couldn't. Even jumping up to a height taller than my six feet. Almost lost my balance, causing me to collide with a burly guy about to make his own way into the pub.

Mumbled my apologies. He gave me a hard stare for several moments, said nothing.

Didn't have to: message received and understood.

As this intimidating character entered The Minerva I held back. For I now knew who this guy was: Lambert Fazackerley.

Fazackerley and his gang were tormentors of the Met

from the late Sixties up until the late Eighties, Lambert being the last of them to be banged up, mainly because of his irritating, but brilliant brief, Belgrave Appleton. Unfortunately, Lambert was a career criminal, couldn't leave it alone: one armed raid too many.

Know he received a lengthy stint inside. Didn't know he was out.

Porridge hadn't done him any favours: his stocky frame not muscular, but flabby, face a grey pallor, eyes resembling those of a pig, spiky blonde hair now silver white. But it was Fazackerley. No doubt.

Know I'm poking my nose in probably where it's not wanted, but... Donegal and Fazackerley together?

Don't like it. Not one bit.

Hunched up my Henri Lloyd jacket collar, pulled down my flat cap over my eyes and pushed my way into the crowded pub.

Surveyed my surroundings. Not long before I spotted the two old adversaries huddled over a small, round table, deep in conversation.

Neither had a drink: sign of a quick deal and away. If only I could listen in.

As I was contemplating whether to move nearer to the pair, Fazackerley pulled out his wallet, removed a large wad of paper money and peeled off £50 notes, forty in total.

Within seconds my mind was crammed full of all sorts of possibilities, none of them kosher.

Donegal grinned, tucking the two grand into the inside pocket of his overcoat as he stood up, firmly shaking the hand of former Public Enemy Number One.

My old governor had pulled some strokes in his time. But this?

Then the old gangster stumbled to his feet, moved towards me. Made myself scarce, watched as the two elderly men left side by side. Followed them, keeping a reasonable distance between us.

After several minutes I had to dodge into a doorway, as first Donegal, then his accomplice, turned their heads in my direction. Luckily for me a throng of tourists built up and I tagged onto a guided outing as they crossed the busy dual carriageway. Once across the road, Donegal and Fazackerley parted company.

Dilemma.

As a long serving copper, split second decisions had to be made all the time: on instinct I plumped for Fazackerley.

He walked towards the city centre alongside the Prince's Dock, made ugly with an adjacent oversized greenhouse – known as a shopping mall.

A sluggish gait: obviously not a member of her majesty's gym club. Wherever Fazackerley was going, I was hoping it would be warm. I quickened my pace when he made a sharp left hand turn past the perimeter of the dock. When I made this turn I lost sight of my quarry.

Damn!

Searched with my eyes the bustling Queen Victoria Square area: no sign.

All this effort. For nothing. Tempted to visit the nearby hostelry as I passed the Ferens Art Gallery.

What am I doing? No longer a police officer. And I am supposed to be here for the culture.

What the heck. Back-tracked, made my way up the concrete steps to the Gallery. Inside I was button-holed by a turquoise clad volunteer, only too happy to swamp me with information, directing me to the room containing Pietro Lorenzetti's seven hundred year old painting of Christ between Saints Peter and Paul. I'm no connoisseur of art, but it was a breathtaking picture.

When a young kid to my left badgered his mother about seeing his uncle's offering in the Open

Ferens Art Gallery, Hull

Exhibition, this jogged my memory: couldn't leave without viewing my brother's entry.

The kid's mother gave in.

I followed them through to the Open Exhibition, stopped dead: ahead of me near the far wall, none other than Lambert Fazackerley.

Up from The Smoke for culture? Hard to believe.

He was talking avidly to some arty-farty type – tight fitting jeans ripped at the knee, clod-hopping boots on his feet and an oversized fisherman-knit jumper, his hair shaved at the sides and back, leaving a sort of Mohican on top of his head; his dark beard giving him the unfortunate appearance of the Yorkshire Ripper. See, even now I can't rid myself of crime references.

The bearded one removed a large canvas from the wall. Not my cup of tea: kind of abstract, conveying a geometrical effect of greens, reds and greys.

It was handed over to Lambert Fazackerley,who, when examining it closely, gave an impression of an eternally grateful Lotto winner. Because of his massive frame he was able to tuck the picture under his left arm, leaving his right free to shake the hand of the bearded one.

Fazackerley brushed by me with an "Excuse me", beaming broadly, but failing to recognise his former nemesis.

I regarded the empty space on the wall. Arty-farty was gone.

Anxious to know the name of the artist, my eyes searched for a gallery employee. I noticed some people were referring to green pamphlets. Approached a lady, who directed me to the gift shop, where I purchased a 2017 Open Exhibition booklet.

Eagerly, I flipped through the pages to locate exhibit number five, the digit displayed under the area which, until Fazackerley had waltzed off with it, had been covered with his artistic buy.

Here we are.

Title of the picture: NEVER BE BLUE

Artist: Barry Donegal

Checked it again.

Yes, my old DCI all right. Gob-smacked was an understatement. Thought about the title.

Well, no blue colours on the canvas... so never be...

Hang on.

*I'll make you happy*
*You'll never be blue*
*You'll have no sorrow*
*Cause I'll always be true*
*And I'm feelin' glad all over*

# AS TIME GOES BY

*Must remember this... kiss is just a kiss, smile just a smile... fundamental... as time... time goes by.*

The words reverberated inside Harry Simmon's throbbing head. He was lying on the cream Axminster carpet covering the living room floor of his riverside apartment. When Harry tried pulling himself into a sitting position he wobbled over to one side, his pounding head hitting the settee.

From his prostrate position he could see that his normally immaculate clothing was dishevelled. Breathe deeply thought Harry. He felt his head for bumps. None. No one had hit him. Why was this little man battering the inside of his cranium with a sledgehammer? Drink? He hardly touched a drop these days.

Eventually his meditative breathing enabled him to stand. Walking wasn't so easy. He lurched towards the bathroom, where he studied his careworn features in the mirror. He was fond of telling the ladies he was fortyish, but that was being economical with the truth by a decade. And the grey hair was something of a give-away, even though his ex-wife thought it gave him a distinguished appearance.

*A sigh is just a sigh... it's still the same old story... as time goes by.*

Harry washed down a couple of painkillers with a generous gulp of cold water, splashed more on his face, then applied a cold flannel to his neck.

He reached inside his jacket lining pocket for his comb. Panic. His comb was there. No wallet. Rushing back into the living room, his eyes focused on his body's imprint on the carpet. Relief. Smiling, he picked up his wallet and checked the contents.

Harry's relief was short-lived.

Saturday night was pay night. The Manager of Howard's Tea Rooms, York, always paid him for his ten hourly piano sessions with two fifty pound notes – one was missing.

*And no matter what the progress*
*Or what may yet be proved*
*The simple facts of life are such*
*They cannot be removed*

Harry rubbed his forehead and blinked. His mind was becoming clearer. As Time Goes By was the final request of the night. From Holly. She had only been at Howards three weeks. A waitress – twenty-one years old, with a degree from York University. I want to be a lawyer she had told Harry.

He knew all about lawyers. Thirty years a police officer. The kind of experience McKecknie, Jarvis and Butler needed. Being a private investigator suited Harry. And M, J and B treated him well, but he had to be his own boss.

For a while business was good. When it wasn't, he thanked his late mother for sending him for piano lessons aged eight, nine and ten.

Harry and Holly; a common bond. Much to discuss back at his apartment over a bottle of Zinfandel. Half way through the bottle, Harry did wonder why an attractive, twenty-one year old brunette wanted to spend some time with him. Yes, she liked his sense of humour: I always like to have Holly in the hall at Christmas! And his anecdotes of his time in the police seemed to interest her.

BUT?

It was only now, in the cold light of day that Harry realised he should have stopped at the half bottle. He should have taken notice of the BUT. Should have viewed Holly through his investigative eyes – as a client.

*Moonlight and love songs*
*Never out of date*
*Hearts full of passion*
*Jealousy and hate*
*Woman needs man*
*And man must have his mate*
*That no one can deny*

Not so much as a kiss to show for Harry's Brief Encounter.

Sunday night – Howard's Tea Rooms was packed out. Was it the exquisite food, or Harry's musical repertoire. He liked to think he added to the ambience. Holly thought otherwise. She was absent. The Manager was disappointed. She'd not phoned to say why.

He's disappointed, thought Harry. How does he think I feel? He doesn't, as yet. By the end of the night he will. Despite the establishment's confidentiality rule, Harry needs to know Holly's address.

6pm. Harry, minus his hangover, resplendent in black eveningwear, sat down at his Steinway. Effortlessly he played old favourites: My Funny Valentine, Making Whoopee, Thanks For The Memory, and, after some hesitation, I've Got My Love To Keep Me Warm.

Harry continued, including Beatles ballads, when his wristwatch dazzled from the chandelier lighting, he was reminded his first hour was coming to a close: As Time Goes By to finish? May help him remember how £50 disappeared from his wallet. Must have been Holly. Had to find her. She'd taken him for a mug.

He surveyed his surroundings. Not many, if any, interested in his repertoire. They were busy enjoying the delights of Howard's varied menu: cream teas, salad Nicoise, plum frangipane tart, washed down with Swiss wines and French coffee.

One last tune and I can get tucked in myself, thought Harry. Shouldn't complain: £100 for five nights, plus food. Only last week it was £50. And that aggravated him intensely.

*This day and age we're living in*
*Gives cause for apprehension...*
*Yet we get a trifle weary*
*With Mr Einstein's theory...*
*As time goes by*

Out of the corner of his eye, Harry spied his old boss, Detective Chief Inspector Martin Rossiter. Looks like a tramp. Either life had taken a turn for the worse, or he was now working undercover.

Rossiter leant on the piano as the ripple of applause died down.

"Long time no see," said Harry.

"You played well until the end of As Time Goes By, Harry. Notes not necessarily in the right order".

"Very funny. What brings you here, DCI Rossiter?"

Harry could see uniformed police officers making their way through to the office.

Rossiter smiled.

"Your manager's been a very naughty boy. Been forging fifty pound notes."

Harry began laughing. Rossiter was nonplussed.

# CATCH A FALLING STAR

Persistent, slanting rain forced people to put up their umbrellas, or, in the absence of one, run for cover. That's what Jack Koffman did, finding refuge in a booksellers, situated in the heart of historic York.

The ancient, Viking city was one of his "must sees" on a list compiled by him prior to his UK holiday, which he hoped would at least turn out to be twelve months, combining pleasure and work.

A week in Yorkshire's capital city was minimum.

Jack, a twenty-four year old from Australia's Gold Coast was irritated by remarks from the British who said things like "Knew you were an Aussie soon as I saw you."

Even more irritating was, they were right: suntanned, blonde surfer, an agreeable honed body, just over six feet tall. Oh yes, and sporting fashionable Maori type tattoos on both arms, which lead to them rarely being covered with long sleeves.

Since landing in the British Isles during the Spring he'd grown his hair even longer, giving the appearance of a Seventies rock star.

However, unlike many of those musical icons, Jack shunned drugs and only drank the occasional beer.

His occupation, personal trainer, kept him in shape.

And, luckily for him, fitness was a growing industry in the UK.

Had no problem finding a niche in a gym in Leeds, where he was living with his grandmother, on his mother's side.

The gym allowed Jack to use their facilities as long as he pulled in regular fee paying customers. The number of private clients Jack recruited was up to him, as were his charges. His clientele over a two-month period had been building steadily, with females (of all ages) in the majority. Naturally, from the full time instructors, there was a certain degree of envy and , in some cases, xenophobia, but Jack's intimidating demeanour kept physicality at bay.

Strangely, he was not given to acts of violence. Although Jack was extremely fit, he was not proficient in any of the martial arts and, in all probability, be worse off in a fight.

He was in no hurry to enlighten the regular staff.

The youngest of three brothers, Jack was the reticent one. Had girlfriends, but never entered into a steady relationship with any of them.

The last one, Marianne, had stifled him somewhat: three years his junior, to Jack she seemed intent on settling down, but, unlike his siblings, he wasn't ready for that kind of commitment. In truth it was Marianne who unwittingly strengthened his desire to move away from Brisbane. Initially he intended relocating to the opposite coast of Australia: Perth. Thinking about it: not far enough away.

So he skyped Gran, who, because she lived alone, was perfectly happy to offer him a temporary home until he found his own. She stressed this last point, recalling when Jack and his brothers, plus two girlfriends descended on her three years previously, ostensibly for a quick visit. Turned into a long, expensive, disruptive six weeks. Gran, in her early eighties, lived in a modest two bed apartment close to Leeds city centre.

Something of a comedown compared to the showbiz

lifestyle of her youth: the fabulous Fifties and Sixties.

According to Maria Moretti: Gran's stage name. In real life: Dorothy Whitehurst.

Late 1950s to the mid-1960s a particularly successful and fruitful period in the life of Maria Moretti.

Married young, two daughters now residing in Australia.

Maria's husband Derek had no skills of any kind. And definitely no talent for singing, dancing and... well... NO TALENT. FULL STOP. Unless consuming large quantities of alcohol at Maria's expense counted as talent.

Foolishly, in the early phase of her new career, she allowed Derek to manage her affairs. A decision which proved to be one of financial misfortune towards the end of Maria Moretti's stardom. However, a champagne lifestyle all the way while it lasted.

Deep down Dorothy yearned for her previous anonymous existence:

*Who wants to be a millionaire?*
*I don't*
*Have flashy flunkies everywhere?*
*I don't*
*Who wants the bother of a country estate?*
*A country estate is something I'd hate*

*Who wants to wallow in champagne?*
*I don't*
*Cause all I want is you*

During their courtship Dorothy sang this song to Derek.

After he died of a massive heart attack in 1971 an army of debt collectors, including the Inland Revenue, swooped on Dorothy's palatial home in Collingham, an attractive village on the outskirts of Leeds.

The home, classic cars, exorbitantly priced artwork, jewellery and other expensive embellishments were all sold to discharge unforeseen - by Dorothy - liabilities.

Maria Moretti was no more. She reverted to her former life without remarrying, bringing up her daughters, the eldest of whom, Connie - named after the fifties' singer Connie Francis - gave birth to Jack in 1993.

In his infanthood he looked forward to visits from his Gran, avidly listening to her showbiz tales of yesteryear. Because Jack never fitted the archetypal Aussie, a sensitive soul I suppose, he became Dorothy's favourite. Plus Jack had more than a decent singing voice. But no matter how hard she tried, his Gran couldn't persuade him to show off his ability in the bars of Brisbane, or even the West Yorkshire pubs.

No confidence for performing, not even sitting on a stool in dim light, playing guitar, which Jack had taught himself by ear.

His able bodied physique allowed him to pursue his love of cycling, happy covering long distances, usually in support of a charity.

Nevertheless, Dorothy was concerned when her grandson told her he was embarking on a two wheel journey to York, reminding him of her own father's demise on a narrow, hilly Yorkshire road caused by a careless lorry driver, knocking her Dad off his cycle. On this occasion Jack bowed to Dorothy's wishes and travelled from Leeds to York via the rail network.

* * *

Jack gazed through the shop window, thinking it would possibly be some time before the rain eased off. Still, he wasn't averse to a good read and headed for the fiction bookshelves.

His tastes varied: thrillers, particularly spy novels, family dramas, autobiographies. And his Gran encouraged him to read novels written by English writer Alan Sillitoe, who, during his lifetime, specialised in gritty, working class drama.

Only one Sillitoe novel under S: The Loneliness of the Long Distance Runner. Jack smiled at the curious title, perused the blurb on the back cover and the first three pages: 'I've always been a good runner, quick and with a big stride as well.'

Comments from the book's protagonist Colin Smith. Usually running away from the law.

Jack though, was as clean as a whistle. But Sillitoe's book seemed like a good read, black humour contained within the first few pages.

He took it over to the till: operator young, certainly younger than Jack; possibly twenty or twenty-one, not quite as tall, pale complexion, sporting a fashionable haircut: shaved sides, tall crew-cut atop of his head, white tee-shirt emblazoned with a logo:

PRIDE
Love to Love
YOU

The young man scanned Jack's book on the till, "Still raining out there?"

Before Jack could answer he was regaled with more 'customer care' talk, "Hope not. Finishing early today and my brolly blew inside out this morning."

He scrutinised the paperback, then continued, "Not read this one. Funny title. Into sport yourself?"

Pauses.

"Course you are. Can see it now. Body-building is it? That will be seven pounds ninety-nine please."

Jack proffered a tenner. Salesman pressed his change into Jack's hand. "Have a nice day."

Jack returned his smile, headed for the exit, seeing

the rain had indeed stopped. After asking someone for directions to the park adjacent the River Ouse he grabbed a break in a nearby Costa's Coffee House. By the time he left, sun broke through the grey clouds.

He extended his gentle stroll along Judi Dench Walk beyond a bridge spanning the Ouse, continued walking through areas of shrubbery and small trees.

Distance wise Jack was around a mile and a half from York city centre; settled down by the river, drank some of his bottled water and attempted to enter a period of meditation.

Then: a text on his Samsung Galaxy. Wondering if all was okay with Gran he viewed it immediately:

Hi Jack, how's it going over there? Been thinking of you. Even considered flying over myself. Skype me when you can. Take care. LOL Marianne xxxx

Why did I check that text now? The day had been going so well. He deleted Marianne's text, shuffled into a comfortable sitting position, resting his arms on his knees and cleared his mind.

Thought he might have slept, because on checking his watch it was past two o'clock. Shifted from sitting to standing, exercised his back, began walking towards the city centre. Been on his feet about ten minutes, passing a sweeping expanse of grass.

Ahead: a group of men involved in some kind of skirmish. Closer, he could see three youths assaulting another on the ground. Jack's lengthy running strides allowed him to reach the group very quickly. The badly beaten figure on the ground was the bookshop cashier.

Jack spoke firmly, with authority, "Okay you guys, lay off. Now!"

This didn't work.

The assailants laid into Jack, who surprised himself by flattening two of the stocky, shaven-headed thugs. The third walloped him from behind on the side of his head, drawing blood, seeing stars as he fell. More blows were prevented by the bookshop man tripping up Jack's assailant and delivering, via a swivel, a retaliatory kick in his groin. With Jack disorientated, the couple laid out by him, now back on their feet, sought to regain the initiative, only for bookshop man to end the onslaught by utilising his martial art skills to finish them off.

Neither Jack nor Dominic - the bookshop man - favoured visiting the local A & E department, where a possible five or six hour stay awaited them, so Jack accepted his new friend's invitation to recuperate at his riverside apartment.

The cool balcony offered stunning views across the city of York, including the splendid Minster. Jack particularly enjoyed watching the river cruise boats travelling up and down the Ouse, listening to snatches of commentary, detailing the history of the area.

Clinking glasses. Jack turned to see Dominic bringing two large iced Cokes to the table. They sat side by side in reflective silence for a while.

Jack smiled, "Thanks again for your intervention. For saving my butt from a real hammering"

Raised his glass, "Cheers mate."

Dominic touched the Aussie's glass, "You're welcome, Jack. But you got in first. Not easy, one against three. So, thank you."

"What is that you practise – Tai Kendo, Judo?"

"Karate. My father's been a black belt for quite some time. I was only recently awarded mine."

Jack raised his eyebrows.

Dominic smiled broadly, "I know what you're thinking. How come someone like me…"

"No, no. I don't think along those lines, mate. I'm not..."

"I'm sure you're not, Jack."

A silence hung in the air.

York Minster

Dominic continued, ”When I was a kid, eight or nine say, I knew. I knew then what my preferences were. So did the rest of the school. People say it’s better now. But prejudice has and always will be there. Growing up for me was not easy.”

“What about your folks?”

“Much to my amazement my Dad accepted who I am. My mother...”

He let the final words trail away. Jack nodded his understanding. “Never forget how you put those guys in their place, Dominic. Anyway, thanks again.”

Dominic smiled his appreciation.

“Made my mind up when I left school that, if necessary, I would be able to look after myself.”

“Nice place you have here.”

“I’m lucky. Aunty Beth left me the apartment in her will.”

“Kind of place I’d love.”

“Have a nosey round.”

“Sure?”

“Sure.”

Jack took his newfound friend up on the offer: minimalist kind of art deco feel appealed immensely. Didn’t want to intrude too much. Poked his head around the door into his bedroom: Handful of photographs on a wall caught his eye.

Wasn’t, was it? Couldn’t be, could it? Jack moved closer. His point of view: framed black and white photograph, circa 1950s of Maria Moretti.

He examined it closely: extremely attractive young woman, a brunette with hair tumbling onto her shoulders, Ava Gardner style. No mistaking the wide smile accompanied with the dimple in the chin. Hair shorter and whiter now of course. The other, smaller photos of her were recognisable, because Gran had them in her collection. Jack stepped back, recalling one of Maria's favourite songs, gently singing it…

*Catch a falling star and put it in your pocket*
*Never let it fade away*
*Catch a falling star and put it in your pocket*
*Save it for a rainy day*

"You're a fan as well, Jack?"

Glancing Dominic's way, "Could say that"

Dominic moved closer to the cluster of photographs. "I've loved her ever since first hearing her when I was a kid. Aunty Beth had most, if not all, of Maria Moretti's records."

Spread out his hands. "Now I have them."

Jack smiled, "I'm in York for a week. But when the week's up..."

* * *

The twenty-mile train ride between York and Leeds didn't offer enough time for appreciation of some of North Yorkshire's most inspiring landscapes. Dominic's enthusiasm matched that of a five-year-old embarking on his first visit to the seaside. Bubbly was an understatement. But Jack would allow him that, considering his intercession in the fracas a week earlier.

Gran was quite amenable to her grandson's suggestion of fan meeting star. Her apartment was only a ten-minute walk from Leeds railway station. A pleasant stroll would have sufficed for Jack. But Dominic's pace quickened with each step. In no time at all the two men were approaching Dorothy's front door.

Dominic stopped dead in his tracks.

"Jack, what do I call your Gran – Dorothy? Maria?"

*For love may come and tap you on the shoulder*
*Some starless night*
*Just in case you feel you want to hold her*
*You'll have a pocketful of starlight*

# LIGHTNING BOLT

Thunder and lightning, very, very frightening: amplified music from his son's bedroom disturbed Andy's quiet time as he pulled on his weatherproof jacket, in readiness for the evening kick off.

Loudly: "Turn it down!"

A return to relative peace.

Confrontation with Shane was not an option. Not after one and a half, unproductive hours spent with a repeat offender earlier in Andy's working day.

He knotted his black and amber scarf, caught sight of his fifty-year-old, careworn features in the wardrobe mirror – rugged, he convinced himself. Others would say battered. His rising jacket zip coincided with a lightning flash, illuminating the bedroom curtains. Then rain, beating against the double-glazing, an accompaniment to the symphonic sounds of thunder.

Shane's sarcastic voice audible through the dividing wall, "Ironic, don`t you think, Father?"

Andy allowed himself a smile as he descended the stairs.

The point of departing. Barring the way: Julia, "Are you mad, going out in this lot without an umbrella?"

Was it too much to ask? A brief respite. Despite the deluge outside.

His wife wouldn`t understand the incongruous peace and quiet of a football stadium.

A voice inside his head, "Occasionally, I think I am entitled to some relaxation. To try and forget the events of the day. Usually, very stressful events."

A silent parting. Finally on his way. Julia was right about the umbrella. Anyway, got to get a move on, disregard the weather.

*And they tell you that there aren't any answers*
*And I was starting to agree*
*But I awoke suddenly*
*In the path of a lightning bolt*

Jake Bugg's lyrics reverberated inside his head – at least Shane had some taste.

Andy hastened his stride, the grey stones in the churchyard alongside him passing quickly by. Ahead, the throng, a black and amber mass converging on the floodlit MKM stadium, clearly visible a mile away.

Pausing to rub dirt from his eye corner was fortuitous. Or was it fate? Because one more pace and the lightning bolt bouncing off the pavement in front…

Doesn't bear thinking about. Andy smiled: Shaken. Definitely stirred.

Always find amusement in adversity. It had kept him sane these past twenty-odd years in the Probation Service.

*And fortune*
*People talking all about fortune*
*Do you make it, or does it just call you*
*In the blinking of an eye*
*Just another passer-by*
*In the path of a lightning bolt*

A voice from behind: "Long time, no see, Andy."

Indeed it was. He had not seen Jonny for… "Must be twenty-five, over twenty-five years."

"Yes, yes, must be all of that," responded Jonny.

Jonny briefly places a hand on his old friend's

shoulder. “Anyway, nice to see you again.”

“Nice to see you, Jonny.”

Unlike Andy, Jonny looked remarkably well for his age, youthful almost. Doesn’t look much different since I last saw him, thought Andy.

An unsettling shivering.

It was a cold night.

All the same…

“What are you doing with yourself these days, Jonny.”

“Been in the Army. A sergeant would you believe|?

“Never. When you say been in?”

“Medical discharge.”

“Afghanistan?”

“Afghanistan, yes. But I suffered injuries nearer to home.”

The nearer the stadium, the more intense the floodlights. Steady rain, shimmering lightning. Intermittent shadows across Jonny’s face. Disquiet Andy couldn’t dispel. He wasn’t religious by any stretch, nor superstitious. Still…

He fixed his friend with a determined stare. The greying facial hair suited him.

Jonny smiled, made conversation. “Walking with you to the game like this reminds me of all those away trips we did.”

“I remember. Good days.”

“The Blackpool trip, when Lynda came with us. And…”

“How is your sister these days?”

“Your sister! Was a time when you’d say, my old girlfriend.”

“Yes, well…”

“You’ve never forgiven her.”

"Would you Jonny?"

"She was your fiancee. You weren't firm enough with her."

"Easy for you to say."

An uneasy pause.

The pair were in the midst of the multitude of football supporters. But Andy noticed he and Jonny appeared to be protected from them by an invisible screen. A feeling of foreboding engulfed Andy, as though he were detached from his body, floating.

His erstwhile friend's appearance had dissolved the usual, familiar, somewhat jocular chatter, which characterised an expectant football crowd.

Andy jumped, felt a tap on his shoulder.

"Andy, where are you? I'm talking to you."

"Oh, it's you, Jonny."

"Of course it's me. Been walking with you for five minutes or so."

Jonny observed his friend intensely.

"Are you all right, Andy?"

"Yes. Yes, I'm fine."

The stadium was now upon them, slanting rain visible in the glare of the floodlights.

"No Lynda in the headlines these days, I see," said Andy. "Is she still married to that two-faced Brummie? Living on Jersey with her daughter?"

"No, Freddie… he cleared off a few years ago with a French girl, who worked at the same hotel as him."

"Ha. Now Lynda will know how I felt."

Clanging turnstiles.

"You want to see her again. Don't you?" said Jonny.

"As if."

"I'll take that as a yes."

Momentarily, both men lost in their own thoughts.

"I have her address, Andy."

Jonny pulled a card from his Barbour jacket, handed

it to Andy, who tucked it, unread, into the back pocket of his denims.

Not wishing to discuss the matter further, he just asked, "Which part of the ground are you in Jonny?"

"West Upper. And you?"

"East."

"We can catch up some more after the game if you like."

Pause... Andy pulled out his mobile.

Jonny couldn't help himself. "Checking with Julia?"

A stupid smile, no response.

A message to voicemail: Be home 11. Don't wait up. Bye.

"Sure Julia will be okay with that?" stated Jonny.

Still as irritating as ever.

Andy, through a forced smile, "Does the bottom of the flyover suit?"

"Parkers?"

"The same."

"Long time since I've drunk there."

West Upper turnstiles: queues.

"This is where we part company, Andy. For the time being."

Jonny turned to join the line.

"Before you go, Jonny, while it's in my mind. Where are you working?"

"HR."

"HR?"

"Human Resources."

Then, a blur, confusion.

The siren of an ambulance comes howling.

*No one blinks an eye*
*And I look up to the sky*
*For the path of a lightning bolt*

Andy joined other City fans in paving the way to let

the ambulance through. A prostrate figure on the ground, his clothing charred.

A plea from one of the paramedics "We need some more room please, ladies and gents."

He couldn't speak for anyone else, but Andy felt himself being pulled away from the paramedics working area.

Inside the stadium, seated, eyes scanning the Big Screen behind the goal: tonight's mascots Dean Fieldhouse, aged 9 - an innocent looking fair-haired lad, and Jonny Smith.

Andy screwed his eyes up tight, opening the tear ducts to clear his vision. There it was – that irritating smile. No question. The greying facial hair, unmistakable.

Turning to his fellow supporter alongside him, "Must've raised the age limit for the mascots, Geoff."

Geoff unplugged himself from his smart phone, "You what?"

The Big Screen: Mascots Dean Fieldhouse, aged 9 and Jeremy Brotherton, aged 8.

Feeling foolish in the extreme, Andy mumbled inanities about the weather. Geoff resumed his relationship with his phone.

One hour into an unentertaining, error-ridden game.

Rumbles of thunder, flashes of lightning persuade the referee to call a halt, hoping the weather conditions would subside. Many spectators left for home, thinking a resumption of play was unlikely. Either that, or they were bored witless. But resume it did, with both teams giving the impression they would rather be in the centrally heated, inner sanctum of the stadium, mochas and cappuccinos affording replenishment.

A scoreless game.

Julia would call it a wasted night, even more so with Andy meeting Jonny, whom she never cared for.

Departing the stadium, Andy forked left for the short walk to the pub. He cut a lonely figure – others with more sense headed for the comforts of home.

He plodded on, nearly there.

A minute or so, then, the much altered 17th century pub confronted him: Parkers. Hardly ever used it. What made him choose this place?

A break in the conditions. That is, no lightning. But a steady rainfall.

Ten-fifteen. Still no Jonny. Andy peered through the condensed windows of the lounge: a sprinkling of customers.

He assumed Jonny meant, "See you outside." But… A swift search of the entire pub and the Gents proved fruitless. None of the bar staff had seen a fifty something, grey bearded ex-squadie.

Outside once more, annoyance set in. It was just the kind of irritating stunt Jonny would pull. That idiotic smile entered Andy's mind. He checked his watch: ten-forty.

Enough is enough.

Before setting off for home he kicked a nearby, discarded beer can, sending it crashing against a bus shelter: a waiting passenger peered around the corner.

"Jonny, where the hell have you been?"

As the man moved closer, Andy could see, although he had a grey unshaven look, it wasn't his friend.

Near enough eleven-thirty, when Andy's Yale key unlocked the front door of his house. He'd been hurrying: the lightning had intensified.

As he pulled the key out of the brass cylinder lock, fork crackling lit up the door's stained glass window, Andy experienced a violent, electrical shock along his left arm. Rooted to the spot, unable to move.

Then: a Jacob Marley moment. Only staring at him through the stained glass window was Jonny, grinning.

Jacob Marley had scared the wits out of Andy, ever since he read Dickens' 'A Christmas Carol' as a kid.

Now this. And worse – Lynda alongside her brother. No grin from her. Only a grimace.

As quickly as the images materialised, they vanished. Hurriedly, he closed the door behind him, seeing the living room in semi-darkness. A sure sign Julia had retired for the night: spared!

Gingerly, Andy climbed the stairs. The bedroom door was closed: message received and understood. On this occasion, however, no guest room. He determined to sleep in their bed - their bed: ha ha, - no matter how uncomfortable he would be made to feel.

As he slowly pushed open the door, a rippled pattern scattered around the ceiling, caused by resumed lightning.

Andy wasn't frightened. But he was disturbed. He scanned the room. His eyes rested on the face of his wife, her attractiveness disfigured by another flash, giving her a demoniac appearance.

A vertebral shudder: Andy looked away.

As the angels parted for her…

*She only brought me torture*
*But that's what happens*
*When it's you that's standing*
*In the path of a lightning bolt*

Undressing was an effort. Falling into his side of the bed, clothes cluttering the floor, Andy wearily disentangled himself from his shirt, flinging it onto the duvet. He willed himself to sleep.

Restlessness.

Thunder and lightning.

Awaking with a start, "Not bloody Queen again. Turn it down!"

Julia half awake, "Go back to sleep. You're dreaming."

Andy abruptly sat up, "Jonny. Where did you get to? I waited."

Then: singing. Not Queen. "Thank God."

Bedside clock: the hour flipping over to six, "Shame. It's too early for Jake Bugg."

*It's another pure grey morning*
*Don't know what the day is holding*

Bugg's words. Jonny singing.

*And I get up fighting*
*Hoping I walk right into*
*The path of a lightning bolt*

Silence. A weak sun breaking through partly drawn curtains.

Bedside clock. Seven-forty.

An empty space next to Andy, a sigh of resignation, no recollection of a disturbed night's sleep.

All the same, two painkillers washed down with icy water were necessary to rid himself of a persistent dull headache before he showered and shaved, ready to face another confrontational day at work.

Descending the stairs, Andy contemplated a talk free breakfast. Surprise then at a meal ready for him.

A thin smile from Julia, "You had a bad night."

Statement, not a question.

Misunderstanding. "Well, Jonny never turned up for our drink, but…"

"I meant a bad night's sleep. Or lack of it."

Mystification. "Not that I recall."

Julia pouring coffee, "Jonny who?"

Tucking into his fry-up, "Smith, Jonny Smith. You

MKM Stadium, Hull

remember?"

She remembered alright. And his God awful sister.

Hesitation.

She sat opposite her husband. Andy looked up. Julia regarded him.

"Everything okay, Julia?"

She steadfastly held his gaze. "Jonny Smith, you said?"

"Yes."

She slowly eased herself off her chair, left the dining room. He'd stopped eating, seemingly unable to avert his eyes from his wife.

Time elapsed. Minutes? Probably not as long at that.

Julia placed a folded newspaper onto the table.

Andy read the bold headline, briefly glanced up, then continued: time elapsed.

Minutes? Longer, as he re-read the report.

Focussed on the article, "It's not possible. It's just not possible." said Andy.

A pause.

Looking up to Julia, "It's not possible, Julia."

"So you say."

A pause.

Andy shook his head slowly. "There has to be thousands, millions of John Smiths."

Julia picked up the newspaper, reading carefully from it, "An inquest into the death of John Smith, an Army sergeant, who had served in Afghanistan, concluded that he died six months ago in his home town as a result of a freak accident, when he was struck by lightning, on leaving Parkers public house…"

She lets it sink in before reading the final sentence, delivered to Andy as she looks directly at him.

"Mr Smith's sister, former pop singer, Lynda Locket, told the inquest that she and the rest of the family AND FRIENDS, had yet to come to terms with his sudden death."

No adequate words were forthcoming from Andy. He was sinking in a sea of incredulity and confusion.

Julia breaks the silence: a judgement.

"It's stress. You should see your doctor."

Andy, staring into a void. "Parkers. Not possible."

Jonny singing:

*And fortune*
*People talking all about fortune*
*Do you make it or does it just call you*

*In the blink of an eye*
*Just another passer-by*
*In the path of a lightning bolt...*

# BABY I LOVE YOU

There I was. In some crummy, seaside resort in the north of England, August Bank Holiday.

Twenty-six years of age, a degree in law, but no work: not since I was dismissed, controversially, from Butler, Bulless and Bowering.

It was peeing down with rain: sought refuge in Jay-Dee's Amusement Arcade, full of a jingle-jangle conglomeration of coin-slot machines and loud music, which battered me from all sides.

'Baby I Love You' by The Ramones filtered through to within earshot, bringing back memories of my eight-year-old self, sitting alongside my elder sister in a cramped Fiat Uno, driven by my father, who, much to my mother's chagrin, insisted on us all quietly listening to The Best of the Ramones, as we travelled up to North Wales every September.

*I can't live without you*
*I love everything about you*
*I can't help it if I feel this way*
*Oh I'm so glad I found you*
*I want my arms around you*
*I love to hear you call my name*
*Oh tell me that you feel the same*

Had a pound or two in my trouser pocket: might as well try my luck. Scanned the arcade for a change booth as I moved further inside.

Abruptly stopped in my tracks. In front of me was the most beautiful girl I'd ever seen: imagine Audrey Hepburn in Breakfast at Tiffanys. Multiply her loveliness ten fold.

"Do you want some change or are you going to stand there looking gormless all night?"

The voice didn't match the looks: kind of deep-throated, north-eastern accent. And she was older than me: a good six or seven years. Still...

"Er, yes... no... that is to say," I spluttered.

A hard stare. "Change? Or not? There are people behind you."

Not thinking straight, I pulled a five-pound note out of my wallet and handed it over. She pushed a mixture of two and twenty pence coins towards me. Smiling, I wandered off to determine which slot machine offered me the best chance of a return on my investment.

Of course, within half an hour I'd squandered all but a pound of my money. In my predicament, money I couldn't afford to lose. But, feeling benevolent, not wanting to weigh down my pocket with the change, I handed it all over to a grateful young lad, who, in common with possibly every other gambler in the arcade, had waded his way through his own allotment.

"One tip though, son. Don't waste it on the grabbers. No chance."

I surveyed my surroundings, trying to locate Audrey Hepburn's change kiosk. Problem was, there was more than one kiosk. After several disappointing minutes, I came to the conclusion her shift had ended.

A young voice, "I won, Mister, I won. On the grabbers."

Looked down to see the recipient of my largesse clutching some sort of orange, furry monster. I smiled, muttered my congratulations. At least someone was happy.

I wanted to meet Audrey again, even though she appeared to be as hard as nails, with no social graces. Moved towards one of the exits: rain had stopped.

Should really think about a room for the night.

I moved outside. The air was laden with a smelly combination of greasy fish and chips, burgers and hot dogs: tried not to breathe through my nose.

If I'd smoked, maybe that would have alleviated the aroma attacking my nostrils. Suddenly, it didn't matter: Audrey, ear glued to a mobile, had ventured outside for a smoke. More of a stunner without the kiosk to hide her slim figure attired in a turquoise pinafore dress.

Ended her call: casually strolled over, thinking to myself, don't mess up this time.

"Typical bank holiday weather," I said off the cuff, without looking directly at her.

No response: I have that effect on women.

Then she turned towards me, half-puzzled, "I know you don't I?"

If only. "Earlier. At your change kiosk."

"Oh yeah," she uttered dismissively.

That's that then. Began to wander off, but, out of necessity, asked her if she knew of a decent, not too expensive B & B.

She shook her head.

I smiled stupidly, began making my way back into the arcade: for warmth really.

After a few minutes of aimless wandering, felt a tap on my shoulder.

Turned to see, unbelievingly, Audrey, once more, mobile in hand.

She offered her free hand, which I shook warmly, "Donna, Donna McQuillan. Sorry if I was a bit short with you."

Her accent now seemed more refined.

"Don't mention it."

The noise escalated: a continual onslaught as the coin-slots, coupled with Motorhead bombarding our ears with 'Ace of Spades'.

She hooked a finger, beckoning me to follow her. I did. We ended up in a quiet back room, a kind of office with a paper-strewn desk and what looked like a high security safe.

Donna seated herself on the edge of the desk.

A brief pause before she spoke, "You mentioned accommodation."

I nodded.

"Think I can help."

Why I responded with my next remark, God only knows. "You mean here, sleeping in here?"

She laughed. "Must be desperate. What's your name by the way?"

"Daniel, Daniel Buchan."

"And where does Daniel Buchan hail from I wonder?"

She's playing games. "From the south by the sounds of it."

She paused for an answer, even though she'd not asked a question.

Felt uneasy, but... "Cambridge."

"University."

"Well, studied law there. But I hail from the city of Cambridge."

Then, as an afterthought, or was it to break the uncomfortable pauses, "And you're obviously a Geordie."

She surprised me with her venomous retort, "I am not. I'm south of the Tyne."

I let it go. A tense interlude. Donna folded her arms.

"On holiday, Daniel?"

Shook my head.

"Working?"

"In between jobs."

"Unemployed."

"Yes. But it's only temp..."

She held up a hand. "Not interested, bonny lad. Do you want a bed for the night or not?"

* * *

Donna skilfully reversed her white four-wheel drive – Japanese, I think – into a spacious, cobbled driveway. Motioned for me to get out. She'd phoned her father during our journey telling him to expect me, that I would be ideal.

Felt uneasy. Particularly as I missed the rest of the conversation when nature called.

Stood back and was in awe of a large, Victorian property facing me, its black front door reminiscent of Ten Downing Street; in fact, was that a white number ten fixed to the door?

"I know what you're thinking. Same as every other visitor."

"You live here, Audrey?"

She screwed up her face, "Excuse me?"

"Sorry. Mixing you up with someone else."

"Really?"

"I know it sounds stupid, but Audrey Hepburn – you're her double."

Disbelieving glance.

"As I said – stupid of me."

Ignored me. Walked over to my side after she locked her car.

"Is this your home, Donna?"

"Heard of Jack McQuillan?"

Shook my head.

"Jay-Dee's Amusement Arcade you were in earlier. And every arcade along the North-eastern coast, up to the Scottish border are owned by my father."

"Jack McQuillan?"

"The same."

"And this is where he lives? And you?"

Nodded her agreement.

"Anyone else?"

"Only the staff. Shall we go in?"

Main entrance hallway was what I expected - palatial.

Donna lead me down a short corridor, quietly knocked on a large, oak-panelled door and we entered what appeared to be a study, matching the hallway's opulence: book lined shelves, paintings of the Hockney school, plus assorted object d'art. Would imagine they all cost a tidy sum.

A gravel-toned, dare I say, Geordie voice, broader then Donna's, broke the silence.

"Good evening, Mr Buchan. Have a seat."

A hand from behind a high-backed, leather armchair invited me to sit in the nearby empty chair.

Comfortably seated, I now faced, presumably, Jack McQuillan: mid fifties, stocky, craggy featured. And a dead ringer for the Scottish actor Peter Mullan.

I smiled at the incongruous thought of Audrey Hepburn being Peter Mullan's daughter.

"I've not said anything funny, Mr Buchan. Yet."

"Excuse me?"

"Why are you smiling?"

I stuttered and spluttered, trying to think of a satisfactory explanation. One that wouldn't offend him. Behind his back Donna grinned at my discomfort.

Eventually, he tired of my farcical outpourings.

"Never mind. Down to business."

Hoped the alarm on my face didn't show: business? What business?

"Don't stand over there like a spare part, Donna. Come and join us. Drink, Mr Buchan? A beer, Scotch?"

"No thanks, I only drink Madeira Wine."

Donna sat next to me on a hardback chair. I looked up, smiled. She returned my smile, sending a tingle down my spine.

Her father wasn't slow to react, "I was going to say 'No vices'. But I can see you are infatuated with my daughter, Mr Buchan."

Wish he'd stop calling me Mr Buchan.

He paused to light a panatela, brushing ash off his blue, pinstriped trousers. I was fascinated by his gold armbands holding his white shirtsleeves away from his wrists, the bands matching his equally impressive watch.

Jack McQuillan appeared to be seriously wealthy. Puffing away on his cigar only exacerbated his gravely voice, "You're an intelligent young man from what I hear, Mr Buchan and..."

"For God's sake, Daddy, call him Daniel."

Daddy's hard look informed his daughter she'd interrupted uninvited. He let the uneasiness hang in the air for a while.

"As I was saying, Mr Buchan, I understand you have a well educated, legal mind. But presently without accommodation and employment."

He paused to inhale, then exhale cigar smoke.

"I can offer you several nights here. In return, you can carry out an important task for me."

Donna had obviously made Mr McQuillan aware of my plight during our service station stop.

Beginning to have an increasing sense of anxiousness. But tiredness and hunger, informed my decision to agree.

Jack McQuillan shook my hand so firmly I winced.

As I trudged up the wide hall staircase the only thought on my mind was sleep. Donna paused at the door to my allocated room. I leaned towards her.

"Goodnight, bonny lad," she said, pushing me away.

After walking away from me, turning, "Piece of advice: don't cross Daddy. He's a pro."

She entered her own room, leaving me... lost for words.

Uneasiness, anxiousness. Call it what you will: it wouldn't go away. And what McQuillan had in store for me, I don't know.

Bright sunlight filtering through the heavy crimson curtains. Rubbed my sleepy eyes, blinked: in my eye-line was a rather, to my mind, grotesque, naked woman outstretched horizontally on a wide canvas. I'm no expert, but even I know a Gustav Klimt when I see one. Whatever lights your candle, I thought, pulling on my Calvin Kleins.

Following a subdued English breakfast, halfway through which Jack disappeared, Donna informed me that I would have to amuse myself all day – 'Feel free to explore,' – father and daughter being engaged on business.

Took the advice and began exploring the several acres of grounds attached to the rear of the house: strange layout, probably not by design, of haphazard, turfed areas winding through woods, bark strewn footpaths, which levelled out at various points after walking upwards and downwards; dotted here and there were rectangular beds of shade loving plants: ferns, bamboo and skimmias.

An unexpected feature greeted me suddenly around one of the bends: heavy grapevines clustered in a large Victorian greenhouse. Sure Jack wouldn't miss a handful of his produce.

The greenhouse door almost dropped off the hinges as I entered. The fruit growth seemed denser once inside, with the juicier grapes near the rear. Through the compactness of the vines and a stack of old gardening equipment I could see timber crates.

Curiosity got the better of me. Warily, before investigating, I surveyed my surroundings, imagining I'd been followed. Added paranoia: hidden cameras inside the grapes monitoring my every move.

Shifted the tools, opened up the top crate, which wasn't locked.

Now I've never ever used drugs, nor seen any. Couldn't say what the taste is like, or the smell. But, tightly crammed inside the crate were polythene bags of white powder: sure it wasn't self-raising flour.

Should have legged it there and then. And I don't mean back into the house. However, my inquisitiveness hadn't been sated. I moved the top crate, which was fairly heavy, to one side and unfastened the one underneath.

Nervous? I was terrified!

Packed inside the second container were arms: handguns and rifles.

It was warm inside the greenhouse, yes. But this discovery intensified my body heat, perspiration forming on my brow. Heart beating so rapidly felt it would burst out of my chest, the pump, pump, pump pounding my eardrums.

Because of this trauma, I never heard the footsteps behind me. Then: a voice I did not want to hear this early in the day.

"I see you're now fully acquainted with our commercial enterprise, bonny lad."

Tentatively, I turned.

Facing me: Jack McQuillan.

Grinning, he extended a hand, "Welcome to the team, Daniel."

The Humber Bridge

# DRIVE MY CAR

I protested. Oh, how I protested. But it was no use. My uncle's determination was implacable.

Reluctantly, I donned the close-fitting, long-sleeved, Lycra vest, emblazoned with a large yellow zig-zag. Didn't exactly match the blue leggings. I looked down in dismay at my luminous, yellow ankle boots. Felt the hoodie mask thing to cover my face was a step too far and hesitated.

"Put on the mask, Sherman," my uncle demanded in his New York drawl.

"Do I have to, Uncle Maurice?"

"Course you do. The outfit's not complete without it."

"I'll look ridiculous. I DO look ridiculous. And quite honestly..."

"Put the goddamn mask on," he said loudly and firmly.

I viewed myself in the full-length mirror as I slipped on the garish, blue-red and yellow hood, with circle cut outs for my eyes.

"Oh, my God!"

Uncle Maurice beamed with what I'm certain he felt was pride. "Perfect. You look every inch a superhero."

"But I'm not. I'm just advertising lousy pizzas."

My uncle wagged a finger at me. "Don't be so disrespectful. I run the most successful pizza take-way business in East Yorkshire," he said, emphasising 'SHIRE' in that strange American speak.

"Then why do I have to advertise such a successful business?"

He disappeared into the next room. But swiftly reappeared with a double sandwich-board contraption, which he hung over my head. Both boards stated boldly in yellow lettering on a red background, trimmed with a blue fringe:

**PETE'S PIZZAS, THE BEST IN TOWN**

Caught sight of myself in the mirror once more. "Oh, Jesus, I look ridiculous."

Uncle Maurice disagreed. "Fantastic!"

"You think so?"

"Sure."

"Tell me something, Uncle."

"Sure, sure."

"You're called Maurice. Your long distance partner..."

"Your Dad."

"Yeah, my Dad. Benjamin."

"Get to the Godamn point, Sherman."

"Why did the two of you call the business Pete's Pizzas?"

"No one's gonna go for Mo and Ben's Pizzas. Doesn't..."

"Ben and Jerry's ice-cream. People go for that."

"Different ball game. With pizzas you need a hook. See, Pete's sounds like pizzas: Pete's Pizzas. Get it?"

"No. I don't get it. Nor do I see why I have to stand for hours on end on some street corner, dressed like... THIS!... freezing my nuts off, adver..."

"We've been through all that, Sherman. When you came over from the Big Apple, I made a promise to your Dad that you'd work. At whatever. To build your character. Give you some backbone. So he can look you in the eye when you return to the U.S. and say – I'm proud of you, son."

"Yeah, but..."

He came up real close to me. "Not idle your time away in bars with broads with no brains. Now get out there and bring me some custom. Bags of it."

I departed, muttering to myself, "Still can't see it. Can't help... surely?... look like a clown. If the folks back home... well, hope they never will."

Stop in my tracks. Why not? I'm outside Pete's Pizzas main store, preparing for a selfie, when this young kid looks up. "Hiya, Superman."

"Actually, sonny, I'm not Superman."

"Look like him."

"Yeah, well I'm not."

"Got X-ray vision?"

"No. Look, if you don't mind, I'm busy."

"What, saving the world?"

"No."

"If you're not Superman, who are you?"

"A Superhero."

"Superman's a superhero."

I ignored him, prepared once more for a selfie. But the annoying little smuck wouldn't give up. "Can you fly? I'd love to see you fly. Bet you can't though."

He tugged at my vest, knocking me off balance.

Struggled to stay on my feet, but I swear the kid deliberately tripped me up. There I was, sprawled out, some superhero! I was mad. Mad as hell: the kid is gonna suffer. Grabbed hold of his ankles as he attempted a getaway. As I got to my feet, I stood over him, holding him down with a foot on his outstretched arm.

"Time for Superhero's revenge, kid."

"Get off me. You're breaking my arm."

"Breaking your arm? I'm gonna kick your butt from one end of the street..."

Didn't finish my threat. A hand tightly clutched my left shoulder, followed by a headlock.

"Right, that's enough," in a flat Yorkshire accent.

"First off, I can hardly breathe. Secondly, that kid down there..."

"That kid down there is my son."

"Yeah, but..."

"American, right?"

"What's that gotta do with anything?"

The guy instructed his son to stand, which he did. His Dad released his grip, swivelled me round to face him. He was a frightening looking brute: all rippling muscle, you know, gym toned. And his exposed arms lathered in tattoos.

Nose to nose with me, "Okay, Superman..."

"Ah, but I'm not Superman. As I told..."

The kid interrupted. "He's a Superhero."

Dad was in no mood for small talk. "I don't care who he is."

After the briefest of pauses, in which I felt sure I was to be splattered all over the sidewalk, he calmly said, "Apologise to the lad."

Only too happy to oblige.

The brute didn't let me off totally. No. Tweaked my nose with two of his stubby fingers. Could have been worse: certainly made my eyes water though. Selfie didn't do me justice.

My first posting, near a busy main road junction, close to a roundabout. Plenty of road users, plenty of customers, Uncle Maurice had said.

First off, I'm just standing there, letting the sandwich boards relay the message. But even though it's early July, a chilly wind develops, making me shiver. Begin jumping up and down on the spot. This causes great amusement.

I follow up this routine by waving at every passing

motorist and cyclist. A terrific and welcome reaction: tooting car horns, ringing cycle bells, even my photograph being taken. Fame at last!

After a while hunger sets in: could murder a pizza. Ha ha.

Seeing folks walking by, eating fish and chips exacerbated my hunger pains. Locate the fish and chip shop – Priority! Literally, I was less than a minute from entering, but before my eyes...

Well, it's crazy, I know, but this is a job for Superhero. Two mean looking, young guys followed this woman, a not unattractive blonde, about forty years old. Carrying a package.

Anyhow, I digress. As she opened the trunk of a large, green automobile – I'm no good with makes of autos. Or with driving – failed the UK test five times. I digress once more.

These two guys bundle the chick into the open trunk, snap it shut. Couldn't let this go, had to assist. Ran as fast as a superhero could, after I'd chucked the sandwich boards. Grabbed the smallest guy - slightly taller than me, but as I drew back my left fist, the second guy took hold of it, twisted me round, bundled me in motor's rear seat, where I end up sandwiched between the two of them. Felt I should name these gorillas: Bluto the small one, Meatloaf his buddy.

Blondie was ordered to drive.

*Baby you can drive my car*
*Yes I'm gonna be a star*
*Baby you can drive my car*
*And maybe...*
*...working for peanuts is all very fine*
*But I can show you a better time*
*Baby you can drive my car*
*Beep beep, beep beep, yeah*

Bluto, in harsh Scottish tones, spoke to her, "Okay, Deidrie, no tricks, or your companion here gets it. Who is he, anyway? Your son?"

"No," I interjected, "I'm only..."

Meatloaf joined the conversation. "Shouldn't have got involved, Superman."

Tried to explain. "People keep saying that. I'm not Superman. Just a superhero."

Probably wasn't wise for Diedrie to weigh in with her dollar's worth, "I've absolutely no idea who this idiot is. And furthermore..."

Bluto blew up, "For God's sake will you all shut it!"

We all shut it.

An annoying hum of the automobile. Jolts when passing over potholes. Otherwise, utter silence as we travelled through suburbia.

I noticed a brown highway sign: Humber Bridge. Not as spectacular as the Golden Gate. Still.

A brief journey through a leafy, expensive neighbourhood ended with Deirdre pulling into a vast car park. I remember it: Uncle Maurice used to run a pizza stall at the Sunday Farmers' Market.

Not too many people around when Deidrie and I, side by side, are marched from our transport towards the Humber Bridge: raised eyebrows, as you can imagine, from some onlookers. Not every day a superhero is unable to defend himself.

I look to the heavens: Uncle Maurice, what the hell have you gotten me into? Plus, I'm tired and still hungry. Must have been walking in my sleep. Because next thing, Bluto has me dangling from the walkway balustrade of the Humber Bridge, the immense brown crosscurrents of the river below affecting me with acute dizziness.

Worried? Petrified!

Could hear Meatloaf threatening Deidrie, saying

unless she came clean about where she'd been planning to take their heroin stash, Superman is gonna take a fall.

"Keep telling you guys – I'm NOT Superman!"

Why don't I keep my big mouth shut?

Whether Bluto lost his grip, or he intentionally dropped me, I don't know. All I know is, the River Humber was coming up to me awful fast.

Closer and closer, as I spiralled through the air like an acrobat, my cell phone hitting the water. Then, unbelievably, my fall was broken by a soft... well, softish landing, on a cargo boat carrying...

Head swimming, jumbled voices...

"Think he's okay."

"Probably concussed."

"Superman can't fly," followed by laughter.

Try to tell them, I'm not...

Headache, confused... need... help...

"Joe, you're the trained medic here. Check this bloke out."

After a while, Joe's verdict was positive: considering the tumble, I was okay. Relatively speaking!

Said when we tied up at Alex Dock the crew would pay for a cab to the hospital for confirmation of Joe's prognosis.

The crew got on with their work.

I wandered off, found a crate of straw, where I lay my head down, content I wasn't jumping up and down like some demented lunatic, attempting to increase Pete's Pizza sales.

Never wanted to be a superhero.

Too exhausted to feel hungry. Drifted off into a dreamy haze. Really must have been exhausted: my luminous watch showed...

Luminous?

Hang on. It's dark. I'm closed in. My view is via slatted timber. And it's noisy, oh so noisy. For Pete's sake. Shouldn't be laughing. I am locked inside the crate I took refuge in. And if I'm not mistaken, this crate is one of hundreds inside the hold of a ship. A big ship! Not a cargo boat. What's happening to me?

Swore after my short spell in the United States Navy I would never set foot...

Oh, my God. Somebody help me.

I shouted and shouted. Kept checking my watch. Then, nearly twenty minutes later, couple of black guys came to my rescue.

"My God, it's Superman," said one.

Tried to respond, "No, see I'm not Super…"

"What the hell..." started the other one.

"You guys Americans?"

"Sure thing," in unison.

"Where in God's name am I?"

"On US Merchant Ship Clark Kent," the taller one said.

"Really?"

"Just kiddin' man. But you're on a merchant vessel on the way to the good ole US of A."

"Seriously?"

I was indeed on my way home. But in a most unexpected way. We docked in New York two weeks later. The black guys gave me enough dough for a yellow cab.

I rode the elevator to the pent-house suite of one of New York's most expensive addresses. Seemed an age before the door in front of me opened.

"Superman?"

"Hi, Dad."

# LET'S STICK TOGETHER

Tentatively, Charlie Westover emerged from the main entrance of Vernon House on the Orchard Park Estate, Hull. In the early nineteen seventies, when a twenty something Charlie was sowing his wild oats, multi-storey flats were seen to be ahead of their time. Now, in January 2000, they were considered a twenty-two -storey, architectural disaster.

He looked skywards, wary of flying objects from balconies, fearful, not only for his safety, but his immaculate attire - light grey jacket over Navy blue silk open neck shirt, tucked into dark grey trousers – being ruined.

Content, he made his way to a waiting taxi, running a hand through his Fifties styled, greying dark hair, his face showing signs of an eventful life, bulky frame testimony to an unhealthy lifestyle.

Charlie's attention was drawn to a nearby wall littered with optimistic graffiti predicting Hull City winning the FA Cup. Smiling, he began singing "That'll Be The Day" then wedged himself into the black cab.

Springhead Pub beckoned, Hull's premier music venue – well, Charlie would think that, his group being resident Sunday nights. But this afternoon, his group, The Four Just Men, were entertaining a wedding party.

*I went to your wedding*
*Although I was dreading*
*The thought of losing you*

Charlie caught his reflection in the cab's darkened window. Was he dreaming: it was his distraught younger self, staring back at him.

All water under the Humber Bridge now: but watching his childhood sweetheart, Shirley, marrying his best friend...

He summoned the driver's attention. "Put some music on mate"

The cab driver enquired of his passenger's taste.

"Anything. Apart from Presley's 'Girl Of My Best Friend.'

The driver nonplussed.

Charlie: "Don't ask."

Radio Three: Charlie didn't know Brahms from Liszt. Brahms AND Liszt, yes. The driver's idea of a joke, no doubt.

Not long before Springhead loomed large.

Charlie was curious. "The music... I don't suppose...?"

"Mozart's Concerto number one in G, second movement:adagio no troppo."

Handing over the fare. "I knew you were Italian. Foreign, anyway."

Laughing, the driver climbed into his cab. "That's right. From Noodle Hill."

Springhead's compact music lounge: set up for the gig. Wedding guests taking full advantage of Happy Hour.

Charlie, all smiles, headed for the overworked barmaid, Sue, his girlfriend: a sort of fair haired, younger Elizabeth Taylor. He couldn't believe his luck when she agreed to go out with him all those years ago. And all because he changed a couple of light bulbs for her: Sue lived two floors above.

Finally he heard her speak. "Are you going to stand there looking gormless all night. Or do you want a drink?"

Charlie, with mock hurt. "That's no way to address a chap. Some would say, a gentleman."

"Some would say. The rest speak the truth. And I've not had an answer to my question yet."

He shuffles uneasily. "I know. But it wasn't February the twenty-ninth when you asked, Sue"

As she turned to the optics. "I'll not ask again."

Three hours later: demands, accompanied by shrill whistling, for an encore from The Four Just Men. A sweat soaked Charlie concurs, launching into Let's Stick Together.

*And now the marriage vow is very sacred*
*The man has put us together now*
*You ought to make it stick together*
*Come on, come on, let's stick together*
*You know we made a vow not to leave*
*One another never*

Charlie mopped his brow. "That was for the happy couple and the good people of Hull. Although, I'm sure Sue behind the bar has her own thoughts on the subject" A pensive Sue.

Linking arms with Charlie, they negotiated the main entrance of Vernon House and made their way to the lifts.

Slowly the lift door opened to reveal two youths sitting on the floor drinking strong lager, empty cans scattered around, spread-eagled legs preventing the older pair from entering the lift.

The spiky haired youth spoke. "Drinkers only in here."

Charlie decided on a light-hearted approach. "We've had a drink. Several in fact."

A terse response from Spiky's muscle bound mate. "I

The Maritime Museum, Hull

don't see bottles."

Charlie's attitude hardens. "We're the old fashioned sort. We drink from glasses and leave them in the pub when we've supped up."

"Well we don't. So clear off," said Spiky.

Sue intervened. "Now look here..."

Charlie pulled her away. "Leave it, Sue."

A sneering Spiky. "You heard the man, Sue."

Ushering her away, Charlie told her it wasn't worth the aggro.

Sue and Charlie drinking coffee in the safety of his flat. Suddenly, she asked, "Why are you so laid back about stuff like that? Those kids need a good hiding."

He smiled. "Because I'm fat, turned fifty and couldn't get used to false teeth."

She tenderly embraced him. "Know something? I couldn't get used to you having false teeth either."

A contented pause.

Charlie broke the silence. "Remember the flash Cockney at the bar supping G and T? He's a musical agent type. Offered me and the lads a twelve month gig in London."

Sue was all ears. "You'll accept of course. You'll go to London?"

"No and no."

"It's what you've always wanted."

"I'm all talk. In any case, I'd miss this." His hands sweep the room.

An incredulous Sue. "This flat?"

"And the estate. Despite earlier. More good than bad. I'd miss Hull an' all."

Sue's feeling left out. "Hull?"

Charlie clears his throat. "Yes. I know I'm going to sound corny now. But Hull is where the heart is. We all, nearly all, look out for each other. And that is why..."

He stifles her laugh with a finger gently touching her lips. “That is why, I’m asking you to marry me, Sue.”

A startled silence: she is astonished, he is expectant.

*Every star above knows the one I love*
*Sweet Sue, just you*

An anxious Charlie, “Well, say something.”

Sue flings her arms around him, holds him very close.

Charlie whispering, “I’ll take this as a YES.”

# WE CAN WORK IT OUT

The flimsy, light coloured curtains didn't quite offer much of a screen against the early morning sunshine filtering through and onto Charlie's careworn features, causing him to blink. He reached out to his bedside clock – half past nine!

"Bugger!"

He was expected at United's stadium now.

He'd go anyway... needed regular work. Not ducking and diving.

Certainly he could earn a few grand a year singing with his group: The Four Just Men. Usually in working men's clubs and public houses at the bottom end of the licensed trade.

He hauled himself into a sitting position on the edge of his bed, rubbed sleep from his eyes, ran fingers through his Fifties styled hair.

As he pulled back the curtains, he surveyed the midwinter scene through his bedroom window on the seventeenth floor of the Council tower block.

The concrete landscape beyond his home hadn't changed in a long time: tower block after tower block plonked between rows and rows of 'rabbit hutches'.

Charlie trudged through to the bathroom. He wasn't enamoured with the reflection in the wall cabinet mirror: what Sue saw in him, he didn't know. Reaching for his razor, his bulky frame hit the rim of the washbasin, a legacy more from MacDonalds and Weatherspoons than Holland and Barrett. Charlie being one of those pro footballers who never kept in shape when his sporting career expired. Maybe career was not the appropriate word. Despite being on the books of a prominent league club in his teens, he failed to live up to the media hype, ending his playing days at the fag end of the English Football structure, where a vicious tackle shattered cruciate ligaments in his left knee.

That was then; this is now: a fresh start. And if he's taken on by United. And if all pans out well. And if he earns plenty of bonuses, then Sue can have her Caribbean wedding. And all because United's manager, Larry Hattersley, saw Charlie belt out his favourite song, 'Hats Off To Larry' in The Roadhouse.

Hattersley, a thickset Welshman, was old enough to remember Charlie's cultured left foot delighting fans, who were often used to 'kick and rush' football. The young 'nearly man' also impressed United's Italian owner, Roberto Puccini, with intelligent after match comment.

By the time United's stadium, lit up with wintry sunshine, came into view, Charlie was running forty-five minutes late for his appointment with Larry Hattersley.

The stadium receptionist, a hard-faced brunette, did nothing to allay his fear of having blown a fantastic opportunity. She knocked and walked through the door bearing the manager's name. After less than a minute she reappeared, "Your lucky day, Mr Westover."

She motioned with a hand for him to enter the office. As he closed the door behind him, Charlie saw Hattersley, head down, writing notes. In his day he was a no nonsense defender who took no prisoners: a sort of Welsh John Terry, with the face of a battered boxer. Within a minute he checked his watch, looked up briefly at his interviewee with what appeared to be a scowl, then resumed writing.

Without looking up, "Sit down, Charlie."

Good sign, he thought: calling me Charlie.

Finally, Larry Hattersley put down his pen. Folded arms seemed like a threat. The silence which followed an even bigger threat.

Charlie cleared his parched throat, "Mr Hattersley, I'm sorry..."

His interviewer cut him off, "Time keeping not your strong point, I take it."

Civility not yours, thought Charlie.

God, it's amazing what a bellyful of beer will do: in The Roadhouse it was all smiles and handshakes and "Call me Larry."

He's probably going to offer me a job clearing litter from under the stadium seats.

Then: the phone rang. Hattersley swiftly answered. That receptionist was right: my lucky day. Because, if the phone had remained silent, Charlie would have let Hattersley have it – all guns blazing. Instead, Charlie relaxed into his chair, listening to the amiable flow of conversation.

"Yes, he's with me now, Roberto."

Pause.

"Of course I will."

Pause.

"I'm sure he will."

Pause… Longer pause.

"No doubt about it, Roberto."

A chuckle. A click ended the call.

Before he left the confines of United's stadium, Charlie couldn't resist heading back to the receptionist's work station, waving his newly signed contract at her, "You were right, love.

My lucky day."

She scowled at his loudness. He didn't care. Charlie Westover was now United's Yorkshire Youth Recruitment Officer. Or, as he preferred to call himself: a football scout.

A fine, chilly Saturday afternoon. A sprinkling of spectators, mostly related to the footballers running around the hard, rutted park pitch. Standing near the halfway line, overcoat turned up to keep the wind at bay, United's Yorkshire Youth Recruitment Officer.

The match nearing its conclusion, the sleight, fair-haired striker, Gary Thurston having scored two goals for his work's team. Suddenly, a hat-trick beckons, but his inability, seemingly, to be clinical with his left foot leaves the opposing goalkeeper with an easy save.

A critical four-letter word salvo from Charlie halted mid sentence by a tap on his shoulder. He turns.

"This is an honour, Sue," he says.

"Trevor said you'd be here. But why you're freezing your nuts off on a windy field beats me."

"I'm working."

"Really."

"My first day as Yorkshire Youth Recruitment Officer... for United."

A beaming smile awaiting congratulation.

"You've lost me."

"In common parlance, I'm a football scout," Pointing in the direction of Gary, "And that lad out there is destined for higher things."

"You mean, Gary Thurston?"

"Yes. With my help. Needs to cut back on the booze mind you."

The final whistle blows. Players troop off the field.

Charlie puts a finger to his lips, "Say nothing, Sue. I'll do the talking."

"What else is new?"

Gary's seen Charlie, heads for him.
"Great game, son. More or less."
"What d'yo' mean?"

The Springhead's customers consist mainly of amateur footballers, eager to slake their thirst.

Charlie at a table, writing notes. Moments later, his concentration is interrupted by three pints of lager being plonked in front of him. He looks up: a grinning Gary.

"I only wanted one, son."

The lad takes a seat, "Yeah, I know. Thirsty work, playing football. And I was at work this morning."

"Tell me, son, do you need to work overtime to make ends meet?"

"It helps."

Charlie closes his notebook. "You've got a fair bit of skill, kid. Eventually, could make is as a pro. Beats working overtime."

Pauses to gulp down some of his lager, "Only two things stopping you..."

Gary wipes his mouth after demolishing his first pint, "I know. Cut down the booze and..."

A swift retort from the older man, "Cut it out!"

"What's the other problem, Charlie?"

"You've got Beckham's Disease."

A quizzical look from the protégé.

"You can only use your right foot."

Gary shakes his head. "Beckham was world class."

Sue nearby, clearing away empty glasses.

Charlie continues, "I had a better left foot than Beckham."

He paused.

"Mind you, I was left footed. But I could use my right."

Gary laughs.

Charlie tugs Sue's arm, "The kid obviously thinks I

know nowt about football."

Sue puts Gary in the picture, "Charlie played in the First Division."

"What is now the Premier League," Charlie added.

Sue smiled, "Course, he was younger. And slimmer."

With arms full of empty glasses, a wicked smile across her face, she returns to the bar.

Four fruitless weeks later, having stood on several windswept, rain sodden touchlines, West, East and North Yorkshire, Charlie Westover was in bed nursing a very heavy cold, consoling himself though, with one in the bag: Gary Thurston.

He checked his watch: five to five in the afternoon. Didn't feel like it, but in less than three hours he was due on stage at The Springhead with his group, The Four Just Men. A long standing engagement he couldn't break: Natalie Porteous' fiftieth birthday party. And she would not be chuffed if Charlie let her down. As for husband Trevor - the consequences didn't bear thinking about.

Just gone eight o'clock: The Four Just Men, minus Charlie, on stage carrying out last minute sound checks. Natalie, attired in shimmering gold, beside herself. Trevor cracking his tattooed knuckles.

A minute or so later, Charlie breathes a sigh of relief, then joins his group on stage. The Lemsips are working and he always felt good, dressed up in his light grey suit, coupled with a navy silk shirt.

He felt obliged to kick off the proceedings with a chorus of 'Happy Birthday'. Natalie overjoyed, whooping and cheering like some demented meercat. The Four Just Men, lead by Charlie perform a Sixties and Seventies repertoire, enthusiastically received by the audience, ending the first set with a belting rendition of 'I Feel Fine'.

A smiling, sweaty Charlie leaves the stage.

Is that a hand waving at him? The waving hand is not accompanied by a smile: Larry Hattersley. He motions for Charlie to follow him outside.

A bitterly cold night. Charlie wipes sweat from his brow, shivers: the effects of the Lemsips are wearing off. Hattersley lights up a cigar without offering one out. Charlie has a feeling that Larry's not lighting up in celebration. Best to remain silent. Hattersley does likewise, racking up the tension.

Eventually he speaks, "Enjoyed your first set, Charlie."

"You've not dragged me out here to compliment me on me singing."

"I took a chance on you. Involving you in recruitment."

"Look, Larry, I know the Thurston kid's raw, but given time..."

"You don't know. Do you?"

"Know what?"

"Gary Thurston has signed for City. And do you know why?"

"But he promised me."

"The City scout arranged a sweetener - five grand. In cash."

"You never said..."

"What world are you living in, Charlie? No, don't answer."

Puffs away on his cigar.

A crestfallen Charlie offers an apology. Hattersley pulls up his overcoat collar, holds up a finger.

"First rule of scouting. If a kid's good enough, bung him some dough."

United's manager turns to walk back inside the pub.

"You're still fine with me continuing, Larry?"

Hattersley, without turning, “Read your contract, particularly the small print.”

Charlie standing motionless, a sinking feeling in the pit of his stomach.

Sue wandering outside for a smoke, a consoling hand on his shoulder, “Are you all right Charlie?”

His eyes moist, “You don’t have any Lemsips on you, do you?”

The Springhead - even more crowded - the entertainment drawing to a close: Trevor helping his wife to her feet after colliding with fellow imbibers; Sue doing her best to stem the tide of still thirsty customers at the bar. Even ‘The Four Just Men’ appear tiddly. Well, three: Charlie’s merely overdosed on Lemsips. He surveys the drunken chaos before him. And behind, his eyes fall on Sue. Couldn’t believe his luck when she agreed to go out with him or marry him: scouting for girls wasn’t his strong point. Snap decision: his final song would be for him and Sue.

Despite protest she stops serving to listen. Through the smoke she can see Larry Hattersley propping up the far side of the bar, hoping Charlie will not say or sing anything offensive.

She smiles: no need to worry. Her lovely, if sometimes irritating, non-committal bloke wrings some comedy out of his situation.

Charlie, sotto voce:

*Try and see it my way*
*Do I have to keep on talking till I can’t go on*
*While you see it your way,*
*Run the risk of knowing that our love may soon be gone*
*We can work it out*
*We can work it out*

# BAD MOON RISING

A bounced cheque. For self employed electrician Steve Brooks, a disaster: a fifteen hundred pound disaster.

Past few months he'd been keeping his head above water - just! Together with a grand saved from alcohol abstinence since Christmas, his funds would have financed a decent reconciliation in the South of France for him and his estranged wife Melanie.

Now, unless his erstwhile customer coughed up the cash, his planned week, rubbing shoulders with celebrities in Cannes, would be replaced with seven days in Scarborough: not renowned for wall to wall sunshine. But if he and Melanie did have to spend time on the North-East coast, she would not accept anything less than the Palm Court Hotel.

"Damn," he exclaimed, bringing his clenched fist down so hard on the kitchen table, the offending cheque jumped, then floated onto the floor.

At the table, around an hour and three mugs of tea later, Steve contemplated Melanie's closing words before departing earlier in the year, "You're a fool to yourself, Steve. You had a wholly satisfactory position with The Council. Now look at you: scrambling around for work. And little money at the end of it."

She was right, of course. All of the Torys' talk of a Northern Powerhouse was a load of hogwash: the streets of East Yorkshire were not, and never likely to be, paved with gold. Not for Harry and his like, anyway.

He regarded his predicament: gone fifty years of age, no pension plan to speak of, no...

Thoughts interrupted by a thud on the hall doormat. Steve hardly dare look - more brown envelopes, that's for sure.

Stooping down to collect his mail: white among the brown. His name and address, hand written on the small, white envelope.

After slitting it open, using his little finger, he pulled out a sheet of A5 paper.

Neatly written with a fountain pen.

The writer: Yours Sincerely, Ron MacCreadie (Detective Inspector, Retired)

A sigh of relief.

He'd forgotten: months ago, probably longer, and fancying a change of direction, Steve had written a handful of letters to private enquiry agencies, asking if work was available.

Melanie labelled him a "daydreamer".

He eagerly read the letter, which invited him to ring the signatory. Steve studied the bounced cheque resting close to his feet. He reached for the landline: a no brainer.

After the niceties were dispensed with, MacCreadie asked Steve if he had any experience of confidential enquiries. Or, if he'd ever served as a police officer.

When Steve Brooks, electrician, replied in the negative and his assignment was swiftly outlined for him, the newly appointed private investigator should have detected the odorous curved ball coming his way.

But his only thought was being reunited with Melanie.

For that to happen he needed to make good the rubber cheque. Sooner, rather than later.

He ran a hand through his wiry, greying hair as he contemplated the alternatives.

Having postponed his forthcoming job until the following week, he closed his front door and, with a spring in his step, headed for his van.

A ten mile drive on a warm July evening, his radio playing...

*I see the bad moon rising*
*I see trouble on the way*
*I see earthquakes and lightnin'*
*I see bad times today*

A catchy tune, inducing Steve to finger drum on the steering wheel in time with the music. But he was oblivious to the ominous lyrics.

Steve Brooks, Electrician, (NO JOB TOO SMALL) emblazoned in dark blue lettering on the white van: one of several works vehicles parked here and there on an architectural abomination created in the 1960s.

Turning off his radio to offer enough concentration for the job in hand, Steve scanned the semi-detached properties a couple of hundred yards away. His eyes locked onto the target: house number eighty-four. He rummaged through his sports bag for his modest digital camera: good enough. Photograph enhancement can be done later.

Eyes firmly fixed on number eighty-four. But after three-quarters of an hour, still no movement. Checked his wristwatch: don't youngsters play out after tea these days?

A vivid, orange evening sun filtered through the white van's side window. Steve blinked: must stay alert. Focused on the house through the camera lens: a hazy image. Then: two female figures sauntering into view, approaching eighty-four.

How old is the youngster? Twelve, thirteen? Possibly. Must be her. Closer and closer to the front door.

Turn round. Need a decent visual: a clear and definitive image, MacCreadie had told him.

Steve, hands trembling: as the girl turned her head towards him, he lost control of the camera momentarily.

Quickly recovering, he frantically pressed the shoot button: one, two, three, four, five, six... slight pause... seven, eight, nine, ten… eleven...

Panic set in: The reversing, then forward moving van sped off...

*I hear hurricanes a blowing*
*I know the end is coming soon*
*I fear rivers overflowing*
*I hear the voice of rage and ruin*

Steve Brooks paced his living room floor. Needed a drink to steady his frayed nerves. Thought about it briefly. Rapidly dismissed the thought.

A cool, clear head was required. The heat of the night intensified. He ventured out into his small, south facing rear garden, sitting on a canvas fold-up chair. Checked his watch: MacCreadie would be phoning soon.

He must have dozed off. The shrill of the house phone brought him round. He paddled into the kitchen, picked up the receiver: the broad Glaswegian accent assaulted Steve's hearing.

All he had for the Scot was a worthless photographic record of vegetation, brick walls and a public footpath: not what MacCreadie ordered. But surprisingly, he didn't lose his rag. Suggested Steve made contact with a Mr Black. The assignment could then be progressed.

Steve followed MacCreadie's recommendation and took a day off to gather his thoughts. Didn't want to stew in his own juice for twenty-four hours. So he completed a handful of "no jobs too small" for grateful, elderly customers.

On his return home he showered and changed into clean clothes. Had no evening meal, because he'd been snacking with several, offered cups of tea during his working day.

Sitting at the kitchen table, Steve focused on the scrap of paper, on which he'd written Mr Black's telephone number, prefixed with 1470.

Reckon most, if not all, private investigators were ex-directory, thought Steve.

Sod it! Get it over and done with. Seemed an age before Black answered his phone.

"Hello. Who's speaking? How can I help?" - the business-like, cautious type.

Steve nervously cleared his throat, "Name's Steve, Steve Brooks. Ron MacCreadie suggested I phone you."

"Oh, I see," - definitely the cautious type.

"Can you help me, Mr Black?"

"Need to know your problem first, sport," - an Australian, cautious type.

Steve explained his problem.

An unwelcome pause.

"Well, Steve Brooks. First off you need to equip yourself with a quality movie camera. Mac's client obviously requires proof positive the young girl resides at eighty-four Orwell Crescent. Best way is to partially conceal the camera in a shoulder bag, knock on the door under some kind of pretence: Jehovah's Witness, say. If she doesn't answer the door, try and bring the girl into the conversation and to the doorstep. Or, you could position the camera on the dashboard of your vehicle, facing the front door, hoping you film the girl coming and going."

"Do these methods work?"

"First one's risky, obviously. Second one's a long

shot – if you'll pardon the pun."

Steve in no mood for jokes. "So, it's one or the other?"

"Could try a third."

"Which is?"

"Establish which school the girl attends. Park your vehicle close to the school entrance. Film her on leaving, drive to eighty-four and film her entering."

An alarmed Steve, "Sounds precarious."

Smith half laughed, "Precarious? Perilous more like."

"You wouldn't do it?"

"No way, mate. Likely to get your collar felt."

Steve swallowed hard, felt sweat on his brow.

"Tell MacCreadie I'm not interested, I don't want the job. I ..."

Black cut in, "Up to you, mate. I'm merely the advisor. Cheerie-bye."

Frantically, Steve redialled Black's number: the answerphone! Cursing himself for being naive, he slammed the receiver down hard.

Restless days, sleepless nights.

Answerphone messages from MacCreadie unanswered...

*Hope you get your things together*
*Hope you're quite prepared to die*
*Looks like we're in for nasty weather*
*One eye is taken for an eye*

Steve concentrated on his work, accepting more and more. Didn't want to spend too much time at home, his van often providing a bed for the night.

Then he disconnected his landline. Mobile number for family and customers only: that's good. Paranoia setting in: there's a bad moon on the rise.

July merged into August. Steve becalmed: after all, MacCreadie had his address, but thankfully, no contact.

Relaxing in his van after working six hours solid, one late afternoon, he eagerly answered his mobile, hoping it was Melanie.

Hearing Ron MacCreadie's voice filled him with dismay, "I have a job for you, Steve."

A pause, as Steve wondered how he'd got hold of his personal phone number: his white van showed his business line only.

A stupid thought, bearing in mind MacCreadie's line of work.

"Thing is, Mr MacCreadie, I..."

"You're an electrician?"

"Yes, but..."

The private investigator went on to explain what the job entailed: whole house rewire, new switches, sockets, the lot. And a hefty payment on completion.

Steve smiled, pen hovering over his notebook, "The address?"

"Eighty-four Orwell Crescent."

*... There's a bad moon on the rise.*

River Avon, Bath

# PARADISE LOST

The Bristol-Bath connection: late as usual.

Thankfully, my hotel was a short walk from Bath Spa Railway Station. I thanked the Eastern European receptionist for my room key, legged it up two flights of stairs to my room, tossed my weekend bag onto the bed and entered the bathroom.

Generally, after a lengthy train journey I preferred sinking into a hot bath for a while. Now, as I approached the end of the seventh decade of my life, it wasn't an option: falling asleep in hot water was a waste of time.

A quick splash. All I needed. I grabbed the complimentary soap off the wash basin, worked up a lather under the running scalding water with both hands and briskly scrubbed my face, rinsing off with cold water.

Pulling a fluffy, white towel from the rail, I caught a glimpse of my craggy features in the wall mirror, features formed, in no small part, by my younger eventful life.

Someone once said, "If you can remember The Sixties, you weren't there."

Maybe Mick Ronson, my fellow Hullensian, of Spiders from Mars fame had memory lapses. I can remember The Sixties. I was there.

Away from my reflection, I dried my face, rubbing excess water out of my greying moustache and sideburns. A long time ago, many moons, I tried to dismiss that overblown, overrated decade, particularly the fag end of the sixties.

I'd come to Bath, partly in celebration, partly in sadness. My first visit alone since the early Seventies, when I met my late wife in this beautiful city.

Late afternoon, feeling refreshed, a small pewter casket tucked under my arm, I energetically made my way through the throng of shopaholics past the Roman Baths, turning into the Grade One listed area of Gay Street, before reaching Victoria Park via the Royal Crescent.

People were beginning to drift away towards the city centre. Fine by me. It afforded me some degree of privacy, allowing me to bid farewell to Danielle. She wouldn't have wanted me to wear black that's for sure. But it was a habit hard to break when attending past funerals: parents born during Edward V11's short reign, which followed the Victorian era.

To please Danielle - she still wasn't dead to me - and as an acknowledgement to my long deceased mother and father, I teamed a black suit with pink shirt and burgundy tie.

Standing underneath a colossal North American Redwood, I opened up the casket slowly, carefully, sprinkling the remains of a beautiful life around the base of the tree.

Danielle and I were lapsed Catholics, hence no guilt concerning the cremation. But not wanting to leave abruptly, I made the sign of the cross, spent some time in remembrance and, low down on the tree, carved a small letter D enclosed by a heart. Rising onto my feet, I sensed I wasn't alone.

"What on earth do you think you're doing?"

The speaker was a middle-aged, ruddy-faced guy, sporting an ill-fitting toupee.

In measured tones, I responded, "Minding my own

business." I began walking away, not wanting to spoil my moments of reflection.

'Ruddy Face', not to be deterred, followed me. "I am a life long resident of this city and don't take too kindly..."

I didn't let him finish. "I'm a life long member of the human race and do nobody any harm. Usually. Now buzz off and leave me in peace."

Standing my ground I held his stare. Being somewhat taller and probably fitter than he was seemed to make him realise he'd taken on more than he'd bargained for. But I wasn't a violent man, even when alcohol was scrambling my mind.

'Ruddy Face' wasn't to know that. My own mirrored appearance sometimes frightened me.

He viewed me with wariness: message received and understood. Turning away from me, he shuffled off.

Back at my hotel, I wandered into the cocktail bar. Before I could order, an attractive foreign waitress approached me, shoved a drinks list into my hand, began a spiel about today's specially mixed cocktails by Gerald: she pronounced his name with a Gallic inflection. Before she uttered this name I guessed she was French. As was Danielle. The waitress's name badge informed me she was Nicole.

All I wanted to drink was Pellegrino sparkling water. Had to reassure it was not my intention to offend Gerald. "I'm sure he mixes fine Manhattans and what have you. However, water and coffee suit me nicely, thank you. Medically, alcohol is out."

Think she understood. But I added, "If you see what I mean."

She did, apologised profusely and, awkwardly, made herself scarce. I did likewise, heading for my room. The intoxicating aromas were making me nauseous.

The early night had done me good. I woke up feeling refreshed. What was the old saying about feeling sorry for people who didn't drink, because when they woke up in a morning that would be the best they would feel all day?

Was a time I believed it. Not anymore... not for a long time.

After breakfast I left my hotel, yesterday's attire replaced with clean denims, freshly ironed white shirt and Navy blazer.

A spring in my step today. I intended revisiting Bath's historical sites, the Abbey first. The autumn brightness was welcome and if it remained until the afternoon, what better than a short River Avon cruise?

As I turned a corner, elevated Georgian architecture blotted out shafts of sunlight. Then, as I emerged from the shadows of Church Street, I saw him: Louis Sanchez. Playing his Stratocaster guitar – the same pale blue one he'd bought in 1968, the year Manchester City were crowned First Division champions. Louis was an avid fan.

The guitar shimmered in the sun. The same instrument he used during all of our recording sessions in London, supporting just about every Sixties group you could conjure up: The Stones, The Hollies, The Animals, Herman's Hermits. On and on – the list was endless. Not forgetting The Jimi Hendrix Experience: bad experiences more like it. Bad influences, bad trips, bad hangovers.

Bad everything. And I wanted no reminders of that phoney decade in Bath, a city that had been, still was, good for me.

Is this Fate? Seeing Sanchez once more. Ha! Not even his real name. It was phoney as well. Typical Sixties Phoney.

Stanley Burgess: Sanchez's birth name. He

reckoned, being a huge admirer of South American football, that Sanchez had a Brazilian ring to it. Personally, to me, it sounded Spanish. Still, the birds seemed to like it. And Stanley's affected accent.

I studied him as he attempted, in a croaky voice, to belt out 'I Can't Get No Satisfaction'. Trying to charm the young girls as they passed by, clutching their Jack Wills and Zara shopping bags. But judging by the meagre amount of money in his upturned cowboy hat near his booted feet, he was failing to charm anyone. He wasn't doing himself any favours by wearing drainpipe jeans and a close fitting check shirt, covered by a shabby suede jacket with fringing hanging off the sleeves.

Suppose I must have been transfixed by this apparition from my past. Because suddenly, Louis Sanchez was glad-handing me, gripping my arm in a way I assume he felt was with warmth, when in actual fact my eyes watered as I winced with pain. His weather beaten face betrayed his lifestyle: leathery, pock marked skin, bloodshot eyes.

As he released his grip, "Thought it was you, man. You were in a trance. Still on the weed?"

I set the record straight as we headed for the nearest coffee bar. Should have trusted my initial instinct to walk on by. Because probably, at some stage during our reminiscences, Louis Sanchez slipped something into my cooling cappucchino: LSD, Ecstasy? God knows!

All I know is, I came to in the Parade Gardens, flat out on the grass, catching glimpses of a vivid blue sky through a crowd of people gathered around me.

Prior to this embarrassment, I only recall an hallucinatory mish-mash of narrow boats taking off from the surface of the Kennet and Avon Canal, flying over my head, crash landing into the weir and plunging deeper and deeper...

*In the deepest dungeons of my mind...*

As I struggled to manoeuvre into a sitting position, the lyrics of Paradise Lost, by the Sixties group, The Herd, reverberated inside my throbbing head...

*I dredge the shadows, try to find*
*A mem'ry dimly lit, a jigsaw piece to fit*
*Scene of my innocence departed*

Then, "Excuse moi, excuse moi."

The voice sounded familiar. And in my semi-comatose state I was convinced I was hearing Danielle.

I heard myself saying, "Danielle, I'm here. Help me."

A remonstration in French ensued, possibly with the crowd looking down on my prostrate body. How long it was after this incident when I finally returned to something like normality, I have no idea. But sitting alongside me, on a seat offering an agreeable view over the River Avon towards a cluster of wavering, bronze-leafed trees, was Nicole. Not Danielle.

I wished my earlier, hazy impressions had continued a while longer. For the truth of the matter was, I had not yet come to terms with Danielle's demise. And when Nicole gently asked me about her, with concern, not in an intrusive manner, I barely uttered a word, sobbing uncontrollably, before resting my head on her shoulder.

Linking her arm in mine, she guided me back to the hotel, where we sat together in an otherwise deserted lounge. Nicole told me she'd caught a reflection of me in a shop window while I sat with Louis outside the coffee bar. She confirmed my suspicion about my drink being spiked: Louis diverted my attention elsewhere. In a dilemma about intruding, understandable after my tactless conduct in the cocktail bar, Nicole decided to follow me instead. Thank God she did.

Because she made me see that, corny as it may sound, there is light at the end of the...

The Autumn meandered into the Winter, which slowly and reluctantly surrendered to the flourishing, green growth of Spring.

I was still in Bath, Nicole by my side. No Louis Sanchez: he was long gone.

But words sung by The Herd all those years ago wouldn't disappear from my mind...

*Once I could love without desire*
*Her glance could warm me without fire*
*Where is the boy I was, who wanted her because*
*She took my loneliness and healed me*

The Lord Line Building, Hull

# THE RIVER OF DREAMS

A tumultuous, sepia stained, swirling mass of cross currents surged easterly towards the North Sea.

This extensive river, the Humber, never failed to intrigue the chartered accountant Tristan Taylor-Brown, particularly in mid-winter sunshine, contemplating the view, as he often did through his fourth storey office window.

He lost himself in the panoramic vista his window afforded, delighted his employer, 'Jarratt, Holness & Haigh' had relocated from a less salubrious area of the city centre, albeit to a modernistic blue and purple four floored misfit.

As for contentment: Tristan had none. Fast approaching forty years of age. Same workplace since leaving school. No loving relationships to speak of. Living alone.

Sometimes, when all these thoughts crowded his mind, spending his lunch breaks close to Sammy's Point, where the rivers Humber and Hull merged, Tristan was transfixed by the murky waters below and felt an overwhelming urge...

Contemplation of his elderly mother, vegetating in residential care, stopped him.

He was shook out of his latest reverie by Tom Holness, asking if he'd completed the audit for Barstow Electrics. Tristan held up a hand indicating five minutes. Maybe a daydreamer, but his work was competent. In fact, his colleagues saw him as a geek. To rejuvenate his image he'd recently ditched his horn-rim spectacles and replaced them with contact lenses, had his floppy hair trimmed. Made little difference: still overhearing offensive remarks, male and female, about his demeanour.

Short walk from work to Tristan's first floor apartment in the Old Town, a walk he embraced in all weather. But on this warm, sunny July evening, particularly rewarding.

It was when he closed his front door and entered his home that disillusionment set in.

Lived in comfortable surroundings. Bookcase containing his favourite authors: Dickens, D.H. Lawrence, classical music CDs, Mozart preferred, although for some perverse reason had a liking for Billy Joel. Tarantino and Scorsese dvds featured on a lower shelf. However, loneliness and little sense of achievement engulfed him.

After preparing an oven-ready meal, he positioned himself in front of the television news, only half watching.

Then: surreal, colourful images charging out of his TV set. Not the actual news – some crisis in Paris. Or was it Belgium? Graffiti spattered alongside railway tracks, on underpass walls, everywhere, in fact. He'd always been critical of vividly coloured, modern architecture. But this unexpected introduction to graffiti was something else. It was art, he convinced himself.

Putting aside his meal, Tristan fired up his computer. He googled graffiti sites until his head buzzed: professional graffiti artists, prison for some of them, graffiti wars, the history of graffiti. On and on, page after page.

He pulled a can of Coke from his refrigerator, gulped half down in one go and brought up his Amazon account on the computer; only this time, no books, no

CDs, no dvds.

He placed an order for a twelve can collection of Fluorescent Neon spray paint (orange, green, yellow, red, pink and blue) into his shopping cart, finished off his Coke, considered for a minute or so whether he was doing the right thing. Focused his mind on the vibrant spray cans: without thinking he'd pressed the BUY button.

There! Done it. Delivery within three to five working days.

Standing on the well worn boards of the pier, which, until 1981, was the departure and docking point of the Humber Ferry, Tristan checked the date on his wrist-watch: another day to delivery.

Finished work half an hour earlier than usual, didn't want to go home. Felt the pull of the river, Billy Joel's song echoing in his mind:

*In the middle of the night*
*I go walking in my sleep*
*From the mountains of faith*
*To a river so deep*
*I must be looking for something*
*Something scared I lost*
*But the river is wide*
*And it's too hard to cross*

The late evening sun of mid-summer was reflecting off the river's stillness, radiating calm within Tristan.

Following evening, minutes after he'd arrived home from work: a rat-tat-tat on his front door. His elderly neighbour, Doreen, handing over his expected box of paints. Artistic utensils: yes, must think of himself as aesthetic, creative.

He waited til dark, then ventured out of his

apartment attired entirely in black, including a plain woolly hat, spray cans tucked into a small holdall.

After a brisk half hour walk, taking Tristan past Dunston Ship Repairers and the imposing brick built, defunct Insurance Building, he arrived at the site of his graffiti premiere: the derelict, boarded Lord Line edifice. For decades it had been slowly falling into a pitiful state of disrepair, which in turn was encouraging unsightly vegetation growth on and around the structure. Situated alongside the Humber, the Lord Line offices had represented the world's largest fishing fleet, closing down in 1975.

Tristan stood back from the four storey high, moonlit building, reminder of Hull's former prominence as one of the UK's leading ports. He allowed himself a smile, thinking affectionately of his late grandfather, Luke Taylor, who endured the ferocity of the Barents Sea fishing grounds as a trawler skipper for Lord Line, mainly in the nineteen fifties and sixties.

Sudden noise.

He surveyed his surroundings: plenty of flat, derelict land, splattered with broken bricks, broken pieces of timber, the odd drinks can. An enhanced wind tempo may have blown a can...

But?

He was here now. No time for indecision, cold feet.

Tristan moved closer to his 'canvas'. Most of the existing graffiti was a lot higher up the brickwork, very little lower down, leaving him plenty of space, although he was amused by sprayed optimism nearby prophesying Hull City winning the European Champions League in 2025.

Unzipping his holdall, he pulled out half a dozen cans of spray paint. He'd sketched out surreal designs on paper earlier. Taking aim at the wall, Tristan embarked on his task. But within seconds his intended pattern didn't take shape. Instead, his left hand, seemingly controlled by someone else, began illustrating a monster of mythological features: lion's head, goat's body with a tail formed by a serpent. Gold, yellow, orange colours prominent.

Tristan paused with puzzlement after completion, at what he had created, then signed off with a gold pound sign inside a circle of the same colour: an appropriate tag. As he packed away his equipment, a feeling of exhilaration saturated his body.

A leisurely stroll home was in order. Turned to leave his artistic endeavours for others to enjoy. He interrupted his stride, aware of the close proximity of someone else draining his elation. The suddenness of this unexpected intruder alarmed him, leaving Tristan drenched in nervous sweat.

A break in the silence, "I've been watching you, Tristan Taylor-Brown."

He moved closer to the voice: a girl, dark, casual clothing, no headwear.

"Who are you, why are you watching me. How do you know my name?"

Despite the close-cropped, spiky haircut, nose ring and lip stud, the girl had a pleasant, swarthy complexion. Possibly mid-twenties.

"I'd expect that line of questioning from an accountant."

Not a local girl, from down south. Tristan began moving away, didn't like this kind of intrusion into his life.

"Before you leave," she said, "You may want to take a look at some photographs."

She held up her brightly-lit smart phone. She had his full attention as she scrolled through around a dozen snapshots of a nervous Tristan, furtively spraying Lord Line's brickwork.

After the film show, the girl snapped her phone shut.

"What is this?" he uttered anxiously.

An hour later, as he lay in his bed, fascinated by scattered shadows on the ceiling created by a gap in the curtains, he reflected on his encounter with Echidne. That was her name, the girl, seemingly sleeping soundly in Tristan's spare bedroom, silence only disturbed now and again by gentle sighs, presumably as she turned in bed. A bed never used by anyone else.

But now... Well, that was the deal: either he provided her with accommodation, or the photographs on her phone would be shown to his boss. And the Police!

Several weeks slipped by.

Echidne felt 'at home'. Not that Tristan was entirely unhappy with this arrangement: she shopped for him, prepared their meals and kept his apartment tidy. Some nights she disappeared, others she was content to sit with him watching TV, or listening to classical music and opera, Orpheus in the Underworld being a particular preference of Echidne's.

Summer merged into Autumn. One particularly cold night, made even colder when the central heating boiler packed up, Echidne snuggled up to Tristan as they sat together on the settee, linking her arm in his. Began telling him pieces of her earlier life in London: aged sixteen she'd had a son, Chimeira, who turned out to be something of a monster. Couldn't cope: his father, Typhon useless. Chimeira taken into care. Echidne became homeless, took avantage of friends' sofas and living room floors, while working as a waitress.

Recently, a friend had moved to Hull. Promised Echidne a room: a promise broken.

She tucked her head into his shoulder. Tristan allowed himself to be affectionate in return, kissing her cheek. Never felt like this before: secure contentedness. Permitted his mind to wander back to his younger days: nothing as bad as Echidne's. Nowhere near. However...

He was, is, a loner. Even in a crowded room, the annual office party, for example, he felt alone.

Kept his relationship quiet at work. Colleagues, though, noted a change. Ribbed him no end.

Normally, he didn't appreciate Mickey-taking, being made a fool of. All he had to do now was envisage Echidne to ward off this puerile behaviour. Felt overwhelmingly fulfilled. Even his beloved river had lost some of its appeal.

Early December. Flutterings of snow. Fluttering in the heart when Echidne told Tristan she wanted to move their liaison forward.

Urgency in her voice he couldn't fathom. She wanted him to leave work earlier than usual: an intimate meal for two. As she kissed him goodbye on the doorstep, his emotions were all over the place. And he didn't know why.

After his day's work was done, Tristan eagerly headed for home, earlier uneasiness having dissipated somewhat.

Succulent cooking aromas welcomed him into his apartment: a table expertly laid in the living room, an opened bottle of Chilean Merlot, a candle's flame casting dancing shadows on the walls.

Looked in the kitchen, bedrooms, bathroom: no Echidne. Her phone went straight to voice mail.

Still wearing his overcoat, he slumped into his armchair near the television. Only now did he see that it was switched on: News 24.

Settee offered an improved viewing position: he moved. Television images seem to draw him inside the set, had no awareness of his immediate surroundings.

He was in Paris. Maybe. Belgium?

Surreal, colourful impressions. Splattered graffiti.

Deja vu – up to a point.

Echidne appeared before him. Desperate, smiling. Then pulled away as Tristan's inconsolable pleas for her to stay with him went unheard, as he unwillingly retreated from the television.

Early hours: same dancing shadows on his bedroom ceiling. An unbearable silence. Tristan left his bed, checked the rest of his apartment: he was alone.

Eight in the morning: misty.

Tristan making his way to work. Changed direction. Headed for the old horse-wash close to the former Humber Ferry Terminal.

*I'm not sure about a life after this.*
*God knows I've been a spiritual man.*
*Baptised by the fire, I wade into the river,*
*That runs to the promised land.*

"Five minutes you said, Mr Taylor-Brown."

Tristan averted his gaze from the window: it was Holness.

"Excuse me?"

"The Barstow figures. You said, five minutes." Checked his watch. "That must have been nearly an hour ago."

*I go walking in my sleep*
*Through the deserts of truth*
*To the river so deep*
*We all end in the ocean*
*We all start in the streams*
*We're all carried along*
*By the river of dreams*

# WONDROUS PLACE

Hunching up his overcoat collar against the bitter January cold, Brian Shepherd looked beyond the weather-beaten headstones, monuments and memorials towards the overcast sky, which cast a carpet of gloom over the western reaches of Yorkshire.

This time of year always brought his old schoolmate, Ossie, to mind, ever optimistic then; nothing could dim his mood.

"What's up wi' you, Shep?"

"It's the time of year – I don't like winter."

That was a lifetime ago, nearly forty years in fact. But now – a new century beckoned.

Shep alone, after the departure of the mourners, viewed the freshly raked soil over his late father's grave, the headstone, as yet, only showing his long dead mother's name.

June, Shep's older sister wanted a flowery inscription for his father etched onto the stone. But he had no time for hypocrisy, particularly in the after life.

"No. I don't like winter," he said to himself.

"They say it's the first sign of madness – talking to yourself."

Brian Shepherd wasn't alone. As he turned, a face from his youth stood before him. Not immediate recognition. But slowly...

"Joan?"

A warm embrace from an attractive middle-aged blonde woman in midwinter wasn't the worse thing that had ever happened to him. But Joan had caught him unawares.

She withdrew several paces from him. “Still as serious as ever, Shep.”

His smooth shaven features broke into a smile, of sorts. He ran a hand through his greying fair hair.

A puzzled Joan. “What’s so funny?”

“You, turning up like this. Out of the blue. In a graveyard. It’s reminded me of “Tales of the Unexpected”.

“The television series?”

Shep nods. “I didn’t see you at the service.”

Joan shuffles uncomfortably on the damp grass.

“Confession. I wasn’t there. I didn’t know your Dad, if you remember.”

“Neither did I. But he was my father. So, you happened to be passing?

“I read in the local paper about your Dad’s passing. We’ve not seen each other...”

“It’s thirty-eight years, Joan.”

He links arms with his old flame, “Come on. I’ll buy you a coffee”

* * *

December 1962: the lead up to the Big Freeze.

It smothered the West Riding of Yorkshire the following month.

Sixteen-year-old Brian Shepherd strolling along the main thoroughfare of his hometown in the early evening. He paused at a semi darkened shop window, using his reflection to comb his fair hair into a quiff, a style copied from his vocal hero, Billy Fury.

He turned up his jerkin collar to ward off the biting cold, continued walking, oblivious to the Christmas decorations: his mood is not festive, having again argued with his father.

A voice from a doorway interrupts his stride, "Got a light?"

Then, stepping from the shadows, "Hiya, Brian."

Shep knew her: Joan Buckingham, her well-developed figure making her appear older than she is, short hairstyle giving a passing resemblance to Natalie Wood, but with fairer hair.

"Smoking at your age, Joan?"

"Sixteen last Easter."

He smiled, fished a lighter from his inside pocket, lit her cigarette. They walked together. She broke the awkward silence.

"Where've you been tonight? Out wi' your girlfriend?"

Shep paused before bashfully responding, "Don't have one."

"Come off it. Bet you've had loads of birds."

"You're mixing me up with Ossie."

A half laugh from her. "Dave Osbourne? That big-headed sod – he's all gob."

Shep smiled broadly. "And you know it," added Joan.

"Ossie's okay – a good mate."

"And mates stick together, eh?"

A shrug.

The cold became more intense as they walked. He knew one thing: Ossie was good at chatting up girls.

For the sake of something to say, "Where've you been tonight, Joan, anyway?"

Her reply accompanied by an exhalation of smoke, "Nowhere in particular. Just moochin.around. Not even been 'ome for me tea."

A refuge from the cold beckons:Cochran's Coffee Bar. Inside, the faces of Buddy Holly, Del Shannon, Billy Fury and Eddie Cochran predominate on a pictorial wall behind the jukebox.

"Wondrous Place" sung by Billy Fury cuts into the smoky ambience...

*Found a place full of charms,*

*A magic place in my baby's arms...*

Shep, holding two coffees, joined Joan at a window table; he tossed her a chocolate bar.

"Thought you might be hungry."

Addressing him as Brian, she thanked him.

"Call me Shep. All me mates do."

"Shep? Sounds like a dog. Like in the Elvis song."

Joan munched some of her chocolate, Shep sipped his coffee.

A silence fell between them.

The bar was thinly populated and they were the only couple: new territory for him.

Unsettling.

If only he could think of something witty to say.

Instead: "Is your Mum still at your Grandma's? Got cancer or something hasn't she?"

A scoffing laugh from Joan.

"That's the story me Dad put about."

She took in Shep's puzzled expression.

"You haven't twigged. She's buggered off with another bloke. Gone back to Bradford."

He felt awkward.

Holding his hand, "S'all right. Doesn't bother me. Good riddance."

He felt better. "Can't be much fun just living with your Dad. Wouldn't like to think I had to live with mine."

"Me Dad's okay. But don't see a lot of 'im. Works shifts you see... wish he didn't, though."

Gazed wistfully into her coffee as Eddie Cochran finished singing "Rock and Roll Blues."

Wandering over to the juke-box, Shep inserted

sixpence into the slot, selected a record and returned to his seat.

A bashful, grinning Shep: "I've put on a record – especially for you."

"How do you know what I like?"

A shrug.

Shep turned towards the juke-box, fascinated as always, to see the automation drop the record onto the turntable: a tinkling piano introduced The Crickets singing 'Don't Ever Change'.

Intrigued, Joan listened closely to the lyrics:

*You never wear a stitch of lace*
*Your powder's never on your face*
*You're always wearing jeans except on Sunday*
*But please don't ever change,*
*No don't you ever change*
*I kind of like you just the way you are...*

The song continued with words of romance. Joan's face broke into a benevolent smile.

* * *

Cochran's Coffee Bar had undergone various makeovers in forty years. Brian Shepherd surveyed his surroundings as he waited for his cappuccinos: not so much a cafe now, more a pizzeria, the pictures of Sixties' pop stars replaced with scenes of Rome's metropolitan splendour.

He carried the drinks over to Joan, sat at the window table where they both faced each other in 1962. Shep wondered whether this had been a conscious decision on her part.

He smiled.

"Piped music. No juke-box I'm afraid."

"Don't ever change." ... a chuckle ... "A tall order."

"Yes."

"But you've changed, Shep. For the better."

An interruption: one he'd grown used to, not always welcome, still...

A plain looking woman, similar age to him, holding a pen and a copy of his latest novel.

"Sorry to butt in... I wonder if you'd..."

"Certainly."

He took the book, used his own expensive looking fountain pen, "A dedication to yourself?"

"Thank you. It's Carol."

Taking his time, Shep autographed his own work.

Always felt strange, unreal, even though he'd written half a dozen novels. As he handed back her book, she thanked him briefly, telling him how much she admired his writing.

"As I was saying, Shep..."

"Money Can't Buy Me Love, said The Beatles. A common enough truth. But..." he said wistfully.

Joan had often wondered if the press had it right with stories of 'northern working class boy breaks the mould, living the good life in London'. Now she saw a sadness in his eyes.

She gently took his hand. He didn't object.

"Don't get me wrong, Joan. The fame is welcome. After all, I wanted to leave my mark. As for the rest of my life... well, where do I start?"

She tenderly pressed a finger to his lips: message received and understood.

They smiled at each other, possibly sharing similar thoughts: their night of passion before the Big Freeze set in left a lasting impression on young Shep. His initial teenage awkwardness hadn't fazed Joan, who, despite being his junior, albeit marginally, probably had experience in matters of love.

Joan jolted him from his reverie. "Care to tell me about it?"

Momentarily, he took hold of her hand: a pleasing tingle down her spine. "Well?"

He ran a hand through his hair. "I was thinking... that film I took you to see."

"At the Odeon?"

"Yes. Remember the title?"

"Tom Courtenay was in it. Played a borstal boy."

"I'm truly sorry, Joan for my choice. It was selfish of me. Not exactly a girl's film."

She smiled warmly. "And that's been bugging you all this time?"

"No, it's something which stuck in my mind. You know, the night after when we..."

A bashful tailing off.

Instinctively, Joan reached over, kissed him firmly but gently on his lips.

"I know. It's something I've never forgotten too."

She relaxed back into her seat.

Shep squeezed Joan's hand, head slightly down and dabbed his moist eyes with finger and thumb.

"Last time we saw each other, you said you were off to London," said Shep.

"Yeah. I went. The streets weren't paved with gold. Not for me anyway."

"Stop long?" he enquired.

"A few years. Lived in Hammersmith mainly."

"Really? Not far from me."

He picked up on her quizzical expression, explained: "Ealing. Not the posh part to start with."

Pauses.

"Wonder our paths never crossed," Shep added.

Slowly, wistfully, Joan responded: "I was never

invited to arty-farty get-togethers."

"To tell the truth, I wasn't mad on them myself."

"But you went anyway," commented Joan.

"My partner, ex-partner, enjoyed the reflected glory."

Then, after a pause, "First partner, that is."

Stuck for a suitable response, Joan merely uttered, "Oh."

An awkward interlude. Shep shuffled uncomfortably in his seat.

"In case you were… are… wondering, Shep, I never married."

"And, you're not involved with..."

Interjecting quickly, "No."

*Her tender hands on my face*
*I'm in heaven in her embrace*
*I wanna stay and never go away*
*Wondrous place*

# THREE STEPS TO HEAVEN

Heavy weight. Too heavy for my fourteen-year-old, wiry frame.

Incessant noise: a stampede?

No.

Running. People running, not horses.

Hysterical voices; shouting.

Too much. Please be quiet, it is a library you know.

Bright lights. Why are they so bright? Don't need to be bright. Table lamps, that's all we require. For reading, you understand. It is a library.

An almighty crash: broken glass everywhere. And is that blood on the floor?

Why am I so dizzy?

Who are these people in front of me? Some in white coats. Men, yes men in white coats. Women are there too. But not wearing white. Light blue mostly.

Apart from the one before me: Hattie Jacques? Surely not.

She is in dark blue, though. Is she in charge of the library?

She's speaking to me, I think. English?

I reply, "I'm returning my library book. Overdue, I'm afraid."

An apology of sorts.

Then: darkness.

Why? After all, the reason we've come to Bath is to see the illuminated abbey.

Don't feel so good: drowsy, sickly, feverish.

A jab in my arm.

A voice, "Count backwards from ten... nine… eight... seven… six..."

A ring of radiance above my prone body. A huddle of masked individuals around me, all dressed in green.

Cultured tones, sounding like the actor, Kenneth More, "The next forty-eight hours are crucial."

Kenneth More: Reach For The Sky. A good film.

I can't. I can't move. And I'm lying down.

Speaking to me? Jumbled confusion.

Don't hear you.

Then: silence.

Don't leave me. I'm sinking. Slowly sinking down, down... down...

Darkness.

Blink, blink, blink.

An outstretched hand clasping mine: the one not attached to a drip.

A gentle voice, "You're awake then?"

Turn my head towards this voice, eyes watering. Not hay fever this time. Tears of relief on seeing my mother.

Feel reassured, safer. Not recovered though. Don't think so, anyway. I'd been ill most of nineteen-sixty.

"Good morning, young man."

That Kenneth More voice once more, no pun intended. But when I looked up, he looked nothing like Kenneth More. More like Cary Grant. He was great in North by Northwest. A Hitchcock film.

"You're an Eddie Cochran fan, Stephen?"

I am, yes. But how did Doctor...

*I wanna stay up all night*
*See the big city lights*
*No more troubles or worries at home*
*Hmm, yeah man, that's heaven to me*

"He died you know," Stephen said.

Mum and Doctor in unison, "Who?"

"Eddie Cochran, in a car crash. Gene Vincent was with him. He wasn't killed."

An awkward silence.

When a doctor doesn't talk, I'm worried. My mother looks up to the doctor.

It's so commonplace being called Doctor.

Everyone has a name. I shall call him Cary. Not to his face of course. Too disrespectful.

He may be an Arthur, or Fred, or William. But Cary suits him.

I don't like the way my mother fixes her stare on Cary. As if for guidance.

Funny he should come out with that. Because all of a sudden, I feel very, very drowsy.

* * *

Sunlight streaming through a large sash-cord window dazzles me. As I turn my head, I am confronted with a newspaper headline :

TALKS TO END COLD WAR.

I look around. No longer in a room of my own, but in a six-bed ward. Two beds are vacant, two occupied by elderly, sleeping patients – probably over fifty: that's quite old.

And in the bed directly opposite me, propped upright on a bank of pillows is a pale-faced bloke with black, tousled hair, styled in a kind of quiff. Laying aside his Daily Mirror, he smiles at me. In an accent which sounds American, he says, "Welcome to the land of the living."

"Is it?" I say.

"Is it what?"

"The land of the living?"

He smiles warmly, says nothing.

"Please tell me if it's not," added Stephen.

This kindly looking man – just like me Dad – never has his nose out of the paper. How many times have I heard me mum come out with that?

An interruption of the quietness by Hattie Jacques marching into the ward, followed by a pale-faced nurse wearing lighter blue: she's pushing a wheelchair. It takes a lot of effort for the two nurses to manoeuvre one of the older patients into his transport, before swivelling him out of the double swing doors exit.

A voice from behind the newspaper, "And then there were three," spoken in a matter of fact manner. Chilling, to be quite honest. Don't know if he was expecting a response.

Truth was, I didn't know what to say. So I said nothing.

It was either the arrival of radiant daylight through the windows, or the effects of my medication. But I drifted off into a dreamy slumber: Eddie Cochran emerging from a damaged car...

*Now there are three steps to heaven*
*Just listen and you will plainly see*
*And as life travels on*
*And things do go wrong*
*Just follow steps one, two and three*

"Wakey, wakey," a gentle West Country lilt. Blinking my eyes, I see the light blue uniform of the pale looking nurse.

"What would you like for lunch?" she says.

"You mean, I have a choice?"

She thrusts a menu card at me. To be honest, nothing takes my fancy, so I ask if it would be too much bother for me to have scrambled eggs on toast?

It's not. She leaves the ward.

"You'll not bulk up on scrambled eggs, son."

Ah, the newspaper reader opposite.

"Meat pie, fries and beans for me."

"Oh," is my pathetic response.

"Are you a footballer, son?"

This sudden rush of conversation, for some reason unnerves me.

"Yes. Inside left for the school team."

"That's soccer. I mean grid-iron."

He tosses his paper onto the bedspread.

"Then you need beefing up. Otherwise, well, you know what I mean."

I wonder if American football's his thing. With him keen to talk about it.

Tentatively, "You... don't... or… didn't play yourself. Did you?"

He sits up straight, leans forward. "High School. Had ambitions to play professionally. Motorcycle accident put paid to that."

A pause.

He does have a look of Gene Vincent. No, can't be him. Can it?"

I then surprise myself.

"You're not... No, you can't be. Not if..."

He's intrigued. "Not what? Not who?"

"Well, you do have a look of Gene Vincent about you: the singer? The one in the car crash that killed Eddie Cochran. He's a singer as well. Was a singer."

"I know who Eddie Cochran was, son. And Gene Vincent."

I've offended him. Gingerly, he gets out of bed,

tightening his dressing gown belt as he navigates a path towards me. He grabs hold of the metal end of the bed to stop himself falling. I offer my hand and he grasps it firmly in a friendly handshake.

"Sammy Salt. And you are?"

I was embarrassed at my laughter.

"Seriously, my name is Sammy Salt."

Felt myself blushing. "Sorry."

Sammy patted my shoulder. "You're not the first to laugh, young man with no name."

"Stephen. Stephen Raymond. Please to meet you."

"Well, Stephen. Stephen Raymond, I think me and you should form a team."

He could see I was puzzled.

"A football team."

He pulled up his pyjama trouser bottoms to reveal long white, thick knitted socks.

"Hospital issue," he explained.

I cast back my bedspread to show I was similarly attired, "Snap."

Our conversation was abruptly interrupted by a booming voice: "Kindly get back into your bed. Now!"

Hattie Jacques, obviously.

Meekly, Sammy did as he was told, but not before whispering to me, "Make a great coach for our team."

I smiled. I was warming to Sammy Salt.

Must have drifted off. But was rudely awakened by the noise of a rattling tin box. Sleepily, I opened my eyes to see a tin coffin being wheeled out of the ward on a trolley by two orderlies.

Sammy looked my way, half whispered, "Fred. Afraid he's gone: heart attack."

Took me a while to get over the undignified sight of a human being exiting this life in a tin box.

"And then there were two," said Sammy.

This simple statement sent a shiver down my spine.

"We need a ball."

"Pardon?" was my puzzled response.

"We need a ball," restated my fellow team-mate.

"Oh," was all I could manage.

"Need to get in some practice. And I've thought of a name for our team."

"Team? We need more players, Sammy."

"Obviously. But meanwhile... Anyway, do you want to know our name?"

"Yes. Of course."

Quietly: "Buffalo Bedsocks."

"Sammy, why are you whispering? There's nobody else here," I said in my normal voice.

Cupping a hand to his mouth, "You never know when Hattie will come bursting in. Or if she's lurking around some corner."

Before I could respond, Hattie did indeed burst in: knowing wink from Sammy. She beckoned Paleface to follow her and the two nurses helped Sammy into a wheelchair. With a cheery wave, he departed.

All alone: a solitary patient, hoping it wouldn't be too long before my team-mate returned.

Whiled away the time listening to the hospital radio station playing chart hits:

'C'mon Everybody' by Eddie Cochran... 'Be-Bop-A-Lula' by Gene Vincent... 'Heartbeat' by Buddy Holly... I drew the line at Ken Dodd singing 'Love is Like a Violin' and switched him off.

Had beans on toast for lunch, read a couple of chapters of 'Saturday Night and Sunday Morning' then drifted...

"Over here, Sammy," I called out.

Pinpoint pass reached me on the left. Turning the outside linebacker, I raced towards the end zone, shrugged off one of the corner backs and scored a touchdown, raising my arm in celebration...

"Hey, watch what you're doing. Nearly took my eye out."

Looked up to see Sammy, standing by my bed, holding a bundle of rags.

"What d'you think, Stephen?"

"About what?"

He tossed the bundle in the air. It was coming down close to me. And as I caught it, I could see the bundle was an oval makeshift American football held together by rubber bands. I pulled a face.

"Course, when we're out of here we'll buy a real football."

Sammy tightened the rubber bands to make more of an oval. Must admit it looked pretty good. Don't know why, but I snatched it from his hands and took a throw, landing the 'ball' on Sammy's bed.

"You son of a gun," he uttered, in a friendly tone, laughing as he hobbled towards his bed.

"Field goal," he said, placing the 'ball' on the floor.

Unfortunately for Sammy Salt, Hattie entered the ward, Paleface in tow. The young nurse couldn't help herself: she laughed until tears ran down her cheeks, as her superior picked up her hat off the floor.

Being a Laurel and Hardy fan, I concurred with Paleface. Sammy did himself no favours by pulling one of his stupid faces. Without saying a word, Hattie confiscated our ball and marched out of the ward, followed by a still giggling Paleface.

Sammy's initial amusement gave way to deflation. I'd never seen him like this, my attempt at humour met with him turning in bed onto his side, covers pulled over his head.

Head swimming, blurred vision: my mother, Cary Grant, Hattie with Paleface all coming towards me.

Jumbled voices: "No worry, Mrs Raymond."

Delirious...

"Effects of anaesthetic."

Ford Consul out of control, braking.

BANG, as I fly through the decimated nearside: Eddie beside me – on the ground.

Gene?

"Where's Gene?"

Confusion...

"Sammy, where is he?"

Someone restraining me as I try... lift... my head... Struggle to view Sammy's bed.

All I see is the Ford Consul.

Cary's voice, "Need to sedate him."

Blackness... Blackness...

Through sleepy eyes: bold Daily Mirror headline – ROCK STAR DIES IN CAR CRASH

Panic!

Sammy's bed is empty and stripped. I raise my bedside alarm. Thankfully, it's Paleface who responds.

I'm dumbfounded when she tells me no such person as Sammy Salt ever occupied the now empty bed.

"You have been very poorly, delirious even. After your operation. You've just imagined it."

I protest, "No, no. He was there. We talked about forming a football team. American football, that is. Not soccer. We had the socks and everything. Hospital socks, that is.

And... and..."

Paleface felt my forehead with the back of her hand.

"No temperature. But you are... rambling. Getting overexcited. I can reassure you though, no one called Sammy Salt occupied that bed," she said, pointing.

As she tucked in the counterpane on my bed, she added, nonchalantly, "The patient in that bed had a normal name: Vincent Craddock. Well, apart from his middle name… Eugene."

Stephen responded: "I may have been dreaming because Vincent Eugene Craddock was the full name of the pop singer Gene Vincent!"

'Teenage Idol' Eddie Cochran Killed in Wilts Car Crash—Gene Vincent Hurt

JUST ONE HOUR AFTER THEY'D PLAYED BRISTOL HIPPODROME

# IT'S ALL IN THE GAME

"Was in."

"Wasn't!" retorted Kenny.

"It was."

"Was not."

"I'm telling you, Kenny, it..."

"One nil to Manchester United."

With that, Kenny flicked the small plastic white ball with enough velocity for it to land on the brightly burning coals of the grate.

Ball shrivelled up in seconds.

"You did that deliberately," wailed his pal Tom Cressley.

The smirk on Kenny Laidlaw's face said it all, a smirk swiftly wiped away by a voice in the doorway, "Certainly did. Saw it with my own eyes, Master Laidlaw."

Mr Cressley moved further into the room, his own living room invaded by his son's extremely irritating friend. The very sight of him annoyed Cressley no end. Couldn't help his appearance obviously, but Kenny's defiant, squinty eyes behind his National Health spectacles served to heighten the annoyance.

Tom told his Dad that his friend's 'pudding basin' haircut was the outcome of Mrs Laidlaw's undeniable inexperience with a pair of scissors.

An only child, twelve-year-old Kenneth Laidlaw was spoilt rotten by his mother, a fearsome motorbike riding District Nurse. But on a regular basis incurred the wrath of his Scottish father,

Duncan, who had re-located to Yorkshire thirteen years hence, after the conclusion of the Second World War, moving from Glasgow to utilise his engineering skills in the aircraft manufacturing industry.

Young Cressley's father, Albert, struggled to find employment on his discharge from a fifteen month stay in a local sanatorium in the late 1930s. The tuberculosis affecting his lungs meant that "doing his bit" was totally out of the question.

Not wishing his severe illness to be viewed as cowardice, Albert Cressley joined the Ambulance Service, providing valuable assistance at the time of Germany's heavy bombing campaign, particularly 1941.

He never spoke of the horrors, which confronted him. And it was only when a tearful Tom returned home one day from school, where he'd suffered persistent taunting about having a "yellow belly" father, that Albert allowed his son to look at wartime photographs of himself and fellow crew members during the Hull Blitz.

The photos were stored in an old Peak and Frean biscuit tin, which Albert kept in a cupboard in the marital bedroom.

A collection of smaller tins containing cash for household expenses were stacked alongside the photograph store. And Tom knew it was more than his life was worth to ever open the cupboard, which had a small paper sign - CONFIDENTIAL - sellotaped to the outside of the door. For when he reached the age of being able to read, he'd enquired of his father the meaning of the word.

Any such arrangement in the Laidlaw home would have been an invitation to Kenny for further investigation. However, corporal punishment administered by Duncan was seemingly no deterrent in bringing a halt to his son's misconduct. Examples of which were numerous.

One incident stuck in Tom's memory: the two lads playing darts in the Laidlaw kitchen. Kenny particularly reckless, intentionally missing the board so he could splatter the wall and pantry door with holes.

Unfortunately, one of Kenny's darts, owned by his father, bounced off a hinge, snapping off a tip of an expensive set of three, constructed from tungsten steel.

Enter Duncan Laidlaw, home early from work, by which time, luckily Kenny thought, the darts were back in their box, carefully arranged.

Laidlaw Senior surveyed the kitchen: dartboard hanging precariously on the wall, adjacent recently painted pantry door.

He paused ominously, said nothing. Let the tension hang in the air. Retrieved his darts from their usual home: a nearby drawer.

Opened up the box in front of his son: at first sight nothing untoward. But after poking a finger inside the box they could all clearly see the damaged dart.

All Duncan wanted was an immediate contrite confession. Two denials of any wrongdoing: Kenny facing the inevitable. He squirmed as a hefty clout around his head followed a twisted ear.

*Fools rush in where angels fear to tread*

* * *

Tom regarded the fire, then Kenny, then his father. One sure thing: the game of Subutteo was over.

Obviously, Albert was in no position to punish Kenny. And Mrs Cressley usually permitted the boys uninterupted play, so was never witness to the bespectacled scallywag's mischievous behaviour: some would say malicious behaviour.

In any case, her contentedness lay in the kitchen.

After careful consideration Albert Cressley came to a decision, "Right, young Laidlaw, this is what you're going to do."

Several days later Tom and Kenny resumed their game of Subutteo with a brand new ball, purchased from a city centre toy-store by young Laidlaw and, as agreed, no word of complaint to his father.

The ball-flicking incident was a minor misdemeanour.

Kenny's exploits were many. And varied. Some would say legendary. Others downright dangerous. Albert Cressley called him barmy to his wife and son. To his mates – well, his criticism was of the factory floor vernacular. But as irritating as his friend was, Tom found him, at times, hilarious.

Other times, Kenny was inordinately ill advised. None more so when he clambered onto the flat roof of the shed adjoining his house.

"Bet I can jump off here, over the path, over the fence, over the flower bed and..."

"Don't be stupid," Tom interjected.

"Let me finish... over the flower bed and onto the grass."

"You'll break your legs."

And so he did. The day before the commencement of a fortnight's holiday in Torquay.

*Though I see the danger there*
*If there's a chance for me*
*I don't care*

Far from being shown any kind of compassion by Mr and Mrs Laidlaw, Kenny, on his return from hospital in a wheelchair, both legs encased in plaster, received his customary clip around the earholes. By both parents!

Remarkably, Kenny rather enjoyed his transportation around Devon on two wheels. Or so he told Tom.

Duncan's view was less than charitable, letting his son know if he ever pulled a stunt like the "long jump" again, he'd break his neck.

Hetty Laidlaw, however, soon relented, showering her son with affection and understanding, deeds which Kenny milked for the duration of their holiday. Much to the displeasure of his father, who complained that continuous wheelchair pushing had damaged his dart throwing hand.

For Tom, joining in with his pal's derring-do was not an option: bit of a "steady Eddie" his Uncle Len called him.

Unlike Kenny's wounding remarks: "scaredy-cat" or "chicken" or worse, couched in language Duncan Laidlaw would undoubtedly frown on.

The insults had the desired effect, because they gradually wore down Tom.

Parents on the Council estate where the lads resided, continuously warned their offspring of the dangers of Setting Dyke, a narrow stretch of meandering, filthy water, ridden with vegetation and sticklebacks and newts, the latter being the main attraction for youngsters armed with jam-jars.

In his sillier moments, Kenny referred to Tom in a more amiable manner, "Come on, watercress. Let's go newting."

This was Kenny's way of dragging his mate to the dyke for a more adventurous activity than capturing amphibians.

A magnet in the area for kids, specifically Master Laidlaw, were the slender drainage pipes, which intermittently straddled the dyke, affording crossings from one bank to another. Walking across these pipes was 'a piece of cake' for Kenny. Despite Tom's periodic warnings.

Finally persuaded to follow in Kenny's footsteps - literally - Tom warily strode along a rusty pipe especially chosen by the daredevil for its extra length.

Idiot was the word Tom brought to mind as his demeanour became unsteadier by the second: foolhardy, Albert would have called it.

Tom did manage at one point to recover when he almost wobbled into the murky depths. Steadfastly, he persevered. Lulled into a false sense of security, he quickened his pace.

This proved to be fatal. And a couple of strides short of successfully completing the walk, Tom plunged into the morass.

Kenny's initial mirth turned to concern on seeing his pal struggling. Putting his pipe walking experience into gear, he swiftly reached Tom, dragging him to safety.

The adult Cressleys were not in favour of physical chastisement, but delivered to Tom an almighty rollicking, grounding him for a fortnight: lesson learned.

Kind of.

* * *

Duncan and Hetty's indignation switched to frantic concern: Kenny missing for close on four hours.

An admin error had assumed he was away from school sick. A bleak February day. Not without reason Duncan wondered if this was another of his son's stunts and questioned Tom: no, he hadn't a clue where Kenny was. Or why he should disappear. And was pretty sure it was no prank. Albert Cressley was allowed to take Tom out of school to assist the Laidlaws in a search.

Albert calmed an agitated Duncan.

Mr Laidlaw wanted them all to probe all known haunts prior to calling in the Police. Privately he was seething, determined to enrol Kenny in the local youth club when found. The three searchers approached Setting Dyke, Tom gazing skywards as a noisy murmuration of starlings took flight.

Accelerated his pace, knowing exactly where he was heading: Rocky. A lofty sycamore tree, towering over the dyke: an incongruous imposition on the landscape.

Tom regarded the tree with anxiousness, thick and gnarled branches obscuring his view. He yelled Kenny's name loudly.

A sobbing, but audible response, "Up here. I'm stuck."

Rocky: the one challenge Kenny had never conquered. Never reached the summit. Tom was fearful, but he acknowledged his friend with confidence, "Don't move, stay cool. I'm coming up."

The upward climb. Not easy, by any stretch: branches Tom thought were firm footholds cracking and snapping. Took longer than he'd imagined. But each foot in height gained was matched with increased positivity, even though a breeze turned gusty, rocking some of Rocky's thinner limbs.

The sycamore's nickname: irrefutable.

Tom was surprised at his progress. Never ventured more than double his own height: satisfying smile crossed his face.

Such was his level of concentration he'd not realised Kenny was within touching distance. Never seen tears in his pal's eyes before.

"What's up, Kenny?" Tom enquired of him in a kindly voice.

"It's... it's the team... They've gone."

"Gone? Who's gone?"

Kenny, stifling a sob, "You've not heard?"

Sudden crack: Tom grabbing a branch to his right, ensuring his body weight acted as a barrier to prevent Kenny plummeting earthwards.

Unfortunately, couldn't stop his spectacles tumbling down the tree, landing with a splash in the dyke. The two lads facing each other momentarily, before tearfully embracing, bonding in adversity.

Another hour elapsed ahead of Tom and Kenny's rescue in a tricky operation mounted by the emergency services, ably supported by Albert, as the Winter light faded, leaving a threatening, mottled blue-grey sky.

The two pals, as a precaution, under observation in the local hospital, their beds side by side.

A nurse passing by Kenny's bed picked up his newspaper and read:

**SOCCER AIR TRAGEDY**
Manchester United plane crashes

*Many a tear has to fall*
*But it's all in the game...*

# PART OF THE UNION

Now I'm as working class as yer average council estate dweller. Know what I mean? No ideas above my station. A favourite with the folks that: never get ideas above your station.

Not only the folks. Assorted aunts and uncles an' all: council house tenants, each and everyone, scattered around various boroughs of London.

Admittedly, I've progressed further than most of my family: own house, bought and paid for, modest jam-jar to transport me and mine from A to B, regular continental holidays and, during my working life, a kind of managerial position. Know what you're thinking: a betrayal of my roots.

Talking of opinions, I'm being bombarded left, right and centre (no political pun intended) by the thoughts of Jeremy Corbyn and Theresa May on the television and radio. Both champions of working people - according to the pair of them.

Seen it. Heard it all before. And as I'm leaning into my comfy armchair, viewing Corbyn rabbiting on, the thing that catches my eye is the vivid slogan behind him: FOR THE MANY, NOT THE FEW.

Why is it politicians, of all colours are under the impression a snappy catchphrase will attract voters?

My mind wandered back to 1970, the year in which I was first entitled to vote in a general election. Labour Party's slogan always remained embedded in my brain: YESTERDAY'S MEN.

These two words headed a poster incorporating black and white photographs of Conservative politicians: Iain MacLeod, Enoch Powell, Edward Heath, Reginald Maudling and Quentin Hogg.

As a twenty-three year old it struck me as being rather nasty, a deliberation I maybe should've kept to myself. For I was employed in a hostile working man's pro-Socialist environment: an aircraft manufacturing industry based in East Yorkshire.

Don't get me wrong, I was no Tory. But fair's fair. To me, a Cockney born and bred, residing two hundred miles north of London, was a challenge in itself. However, I had no choice in the matter, or did I? Because the old man uprooted the family: him, along with my Mum, me and my younger brother.

I'd had six months on permanent nights: great bunch of lads, including foreman Ben, a genial chap in his late thirties, who did the right thing by you, if you worked hard on your twelve hour shift. Working hard meant bonus earnings. Not everyone's idea of fun being hunched over a capstan lathe beyond the midnight hour. But, being young and single, having a few bob in yer sky rocket made my world go round.

Every geezer on nights got stuck in, toiled in unison: no demarcation lines and, apart from a few old stagers, no trade union membership. Not that I was averse to subscribing to the Amalgamated Engineering Union. It was just - no one mentioned it. Mind you, there was the odd blip in the camaraderie. One which left an unsavoury taste in the north and south happened midnight, Bonfire Night 1969. Never forgot it. About to leave my machine for the canteen, felt inside pocket of my jacket hanging nearby and... no money!

Someone had nicked it. Probably during one of my toilet breaks. Couldn't prove who'd carried out this dastardly deed. But Tony (had this sneaky,whispy moustache) next lathe along, was favourite. He was one of seven unscrupulous brothers: the Dohertys. Storytellers and rogues, one and all. Tony even reckoned he was related to Tommy Doherty. You know, the football manager.

"Yeah, right. And I'm Prince Charles' long lost brother," I told him.

Regards my missing dosh, he spread his hands, put on that angelic face he used to charm the birds and said to me, in a convincing manner I must admit "Would I, Terry?"

Made me feel bad for even considering he'd been the thief. Oh, in case you're wondering, Terry isn't my actual name. No, he figured I was a dead ringer for Terence Stamp. The actor. Wasn't going to argue with that, even though females of my acquaintance could see no resemblance.

Name on my birth certificate is Bernard. Not what I'd've chosen myself. Unaware of other Bernards during the Sixties, apart from Bernard Shwartz. And he changed his name to Tony Curtis. Actors can do that you see. Think my Mum chose my Christian name so she could impress her friends and always pronounced Bernard the French way: Ber-nard. Prefer Bernie myself. Know what I mean?

Yeah, he was a right sort Tony. No animal lover either; take the night a few of us were sat on sacks, eating our sandwiches (couldn't afford the canteen every night) and this inquisitive little mouse came sniffing around. All of a sudden Tony wangs a bloody big lump of metal at it. Whether it escaped unscathed or not I don't know. But I never did see that mouse again.

Funny thing is, was told years later (don't take this as gospel) Tony became an RSPCA Inspector.

Anyway, I digress.

Summer 1970 saw me switch from nights to day

shifts.

I know, I've been rambling on how great nights were: the camaraderie and everything (walking money and mouse slaying apart) but I had to free up ALL my nights.

Why you ask?

Lee. My best mate. Or hoped he was. Yeah, it was Lee who made me realise I'd have peace of mind on days.

He'd been telling me for weeks that on Thursday night visits to the local dance hall, The Majestic, he'd enjoyed dancing with my girlfriend Mildred (loved her name as much as I did mine) plus cosy little chats with her.

Could've been winding me up. Know what I mean?

Question was: could I trust him to? ...well, you know.

NO I BLOODY COULD NOT!

First day shift: flipping nightmare. Ha ha: nightmare on days.

Young kid on lathe adjacent mine friendly enough: Gareth, tall, sandy haired, eighteen years old. Floppy hair apart, his features were that of a youthful John Wayne. Told him so. Also let him know I was Terence Stamp. Both had a laugh. But it was alright by me if he called me Bernie. And us two film stars had similar tastes in music: Simon and Garfunkel in particular.

I am just a poor boy (I sang) Harry joined me:

*Though my story's seldom told*
*I have squandered my resistance*
*For a pocketful of mumbles*
*Such are promises*
*All lies and jest*
*Still, a man hears what he wants to hear...*

"I don't want to hear any more. So pack it in. And get on with your work."

We both stopped singing, turned to see the owner of the admonishing voice.

"Sorry, Mr Robredo," Gareth said meekly.

"Bloody hell. Who was that?" I exclaimed, as Robredo departed. A middle-aged, short, bald, bespectacled man, sporting a charge-hand's white coat trimmed with a dark blue collar and cuffs.

"Charge-hand Robredo," whispered Gareth. Although why he spoke quietly I don't know. 'Cos nobody would've heard him over the din of the machines.

"No bloody civility. That's for sure."

"Be careful Bernie. He's a better friend than enemy."

"Is he?"

We both continued our work. Mine was a particularly messy job, resulting in cooling milk and oil splattering my face and shirt. Wasn't one for overalls. Not like the time-served geezers. Overalls had a tendency to make you sweat.

Pressed the stop button on my lathe, made my way over to the washing facilities. Glanced backwards: Harry still operating his lathe, but giving me some sort of hand signal. My priority though, was to clean all the muck and grime from my arms and hands, as well as rinse out a splodge of oil from the corner of my left eye.

First off, I lathered myself with Swarfega, a greasy kind of industrial skin cleanser. As I rubbed off excess gunge and wiped the skin with a clean rag I heard a false cough behind my back. Turning, I was face to face with Robredo, a sarcastic smirk across his boat race. He cupped a hand to one of his misshapen ears. Began speaking in a clever, clever fashion.

"Is my hearing going? Or did I hear the bell signifying a meal break?"

"Thing is Mr Robredo, on nights we usually..."

Didn't let me finish: surprise, surprise. He came up real close to me, trying hard to match my five foot-ten height, so we could be nose to nose. Made it even harder for him by lifting my heels.

"Thing is, Slater, you're not on effing nights now."

Pointed in direction of the rows of machines. "Get back to your effing lathe. Now!"

I was not given to violence. But that precise moment has stayed in my memory forever. And looking back, sometimes, I've wished I'd flattened the little pillock. Instant dismissal, granted. Little did I realise, dismissal was inevitable.

Heads swivelled when Robredo barked out his instruction. By the time I reached my lathe the bell sounded for the start of the tea break. That little bleeder Robredo hurried towards me, breathless on arriving at my work area.

Then, pitching his ugly round face towards mine, said "Now you can go and wash your hands."

Just like that, sarcastic as you like.

At the wash-hand basin, derogatory anti Robredo comments abounded. Didn't become involved.

Approaching lunchtime Gareth turned to me, "Bernie, know you don't..."

"I know: Robredo would be a better friend. Don't think that's going to happen."

Mid afternoon.

Looked at my next job. Issued by Robredo: screw threading fifty bolts. A bugger of a job anytime. Especially for a semi-skilled man like me. Tried hard to negotiate a beneficial time for the job with Adlard, the rate-fixer: nothing doing. So next to nothing in bonus.

Found out later Adlard, a forty-something, short back and sides double for a German Gestapo Officer, was Robredo's hatchet man, under strict orders to clamp down on troublemakers. In other words, force out those Robredo took a dislike to, regardless of their value to the company.

The remainder of my first week on days panned out exactly as I expected: next to bugger-all earned in bonus. Normally, I looked forward to weekends enormously. Not having to work nights should have seen me refreshed, raring to go. My moroseness was duly noted by my folks. And Mildred. Or Millie, as she now liked to be called.

Robredo was getting under my skin.

Second week on the day shift: couldn't be worse. Could it? Not been grafting more than forty minutes when this burly, shaven headed bruiser, wearing a plain white coat, sleeves rolled up interrupted my concentration.

"Can I have a word, brother?" said in a growly voice.

"Now what?"

I hit the stop button, faced him.

"You've been with us a week, brother and it's been noted you've not, as yet, submitted your application to join the AEU."

This was expressed in a somewhat threatening tone, heavily laced with a Merseyside accent.

I paused before replying, "First off, I'm not your brother. Secondly, we all rubbed along quite nicely on nights without being union members. And last..."

Last of all, I didn't think it was in my best interests to deliver a tirade of abuse in the direction of Vic Quigley, AEU shop steward. Now within breathing distance, his tattooed arms resting on my workbench.

At close quarters, Vic appeared even more intimidating. And I think he deliberately let a period of silence linger. After what seemed like a full day shift, he produced a sheet of white paper from a pocket and placed it carefully on my bench.

"I'll be back after lunch to collect the signed application form."

A sort of menacing half smile played on his face as he walked away with a swagger.

*Now I'm a union man*
*Amazed at what I am*
*I say what I think*
*That the company stinks*
*Yes I'm a union man*

A nervous Gareth glanced my way, about to put in his two penneth, thought better of it and recommenced chamfering his bag of three inch bolts.

Felt tension in the air as the rest of the morning passed by.

Lunched alone alongside my workbench on cheese and tomato sandwiches.

Think I've said before, I am not anti union - not by any stretch – know what I mean? But...

But what?

Why didn't I just sign the bloody form?

S'pose when it comes down to it, I don't appreciate heavy arm tactics, being pressurised.

Chucked a half eaten sandwich beyond my lathe for the mice; picked up my Daily Mirror, flicked through it with little enthusiasm. Although one report did bring a smile to my face:

British Prime Minister hit by flying egg.

The Prime Minister, Harold Wilson, has been hit in the face with an egg thrown by a Young Conservative demonstrator. The raw egg, thrown at close range, hit him in the forehead and bounced onto his jacket where it broke.

After reading the World Cup match report on

England's failure to beat Brazil, I left the newspaper on Harry's workbench.

Then after working for around twenty minutes, out of my eye corner I viewed Quigley marching towards me.

He picked up the AEU application, glowered, "You've not signed it."

Maybe my response was rather sarcastic, for a man of his temperament, "Not had chance to read it, Mr Quigley."

"Are you taking the Michael?"

"No, it's just that..."

He left the form with a parting shot, "I'll be back at four to pick up your signed application."

Vic Quigley's statement was the clincher for me. To say he was less than impressed by my refusal to be bullied into joining the AEU was to make light of the situation. Call me naive, but I wasn't prepared for the following day's scenario: as one of thousands teeming through the factory gates I felt like the Invisible Man.

Within minutes of starting my lathe I realised no one, not even Gareth, was communicating with me. In other words, I'd been sent to Coventry.

*In restless dreams I walked alone*
*Narrow streets of cobblestone*
*'neath the halo of street lamp*
*I turned my collar to the cold and damp*
*When my eyes were stabbed by the flash*
*of a neon light*
*That split the night*
*And touched the sound of silence*

Not even Adlard would converse with me. So my bonus was buggered. Harry furtively cast a sympathetic smile in my direction occasionally. That was it.

Question was: how long could I survive on my own?

That night I talked over my predicament with Millie.

Left me Dad out of it: he was involved in more strikes than a box of Swan Vestas matches.

Millie called Quigley and the rest of them idiots. Adding that I was an even bigger idiot, saying I should swallow my pride and join the union.

Next day: as I set my lathe up for another shift I fixed my gaze on the AEU application, resting where Quigley left it, on my workbench.

Sod it, I thought. Why give myself continuing grief?

Pen in hand.

Then: a lone singing voice behind me.

*As a union man I'm wise*
*To the lies of the company spies*
*And I don't get fooled*
*By the factory rules*
*Course I always read between the lines*

Turned: a cloth capped bloke toddling away from me. Pretty sure he was gesturing at me two-finger style behind his back.

Dug in my heels for the rest of the week. Didn't appreciate being shunned by one and all. But...

"But what?" Millie said to me Friday night down the pub.

"Don't like being threatened. That's what," I replied.

"You've been threatened?" she said with some concern.

Unfortunately, for me, the old man was listening in on our chat. In no uncertain manner, he told me to bring the stand-off to a conclusion.

As I cycled to work on the Monday morning, I couldn't get rid of the twisted knot in my stomach. Know what I mean?

Looking ahead to numerous Mondays til Christmas, I got to thinking what a thoroughly miserable time I'd have.

Trudged towards my lathe. Gareth had already commenced working. Said nothing. Couldn't really. Could he? Otherwise he'd have ended up in the same boat as me.

Surveyed my noise-ridden surroundings: a few operators looked my way, but swiftly put their heads down, not wanting to incur the wrath of Vic Quigley. Speaking of which, the unconcerned shop steward was about to pass my workspace.

"Vic, have you a pen?" I said reluctantly.

*When we meet in the local hall*
*I'll be voting with them all*
*With a hell, of a shout*
*It's out brothers out*
*And the rise of the company's fall*

*Oh, you don't get me*
*I'm part of the union*

Pats on the back all round, pints in the pub I'm bound. No silence now, just sound.

"Don't forget though: subs are due. And for a month it's just a pound," said Quigley.

Everyone's mate now. So why do I feel unsettled?

Ah well, it's good to talk. And for a couple of weeks all was fine. Until!

An apoplectic Robredo strode purposefully in my direction, "It was you, Slater. It was you, wasn't it?"

Didn't know.

On my life, I did not know what the hell he was going on about. Got the distinct feeling others did, judging by the smirks and sniggers behind Robredo.

Turned out the previous lunchtime some of the chargehand's adversaries went down to his house, which sat in a solid Labour supporting area, and erected, between his front bay windows, a white banner emblazoned in dark blue capital letters with the legend:

VOTE HEATH.

The 1970 General Election was days away. Apparently, no one knew for certain of Robredo's voting preference.

A rumour: he was indeed an advocate of the Tory Party.

Bloody marvellous how life turns out. Know what I mean? I'd extracted myself satisfactorily from the trade union imbroglio. Now this.

Wasn't looking good. Because Robredo was a big chum of the foreman, Fred Waterman, who wielded all the power in the shed where I worked.

Thing was, Waterman was, like me, a Londoner. That should have gone in my favour. However, found out later he hailed from West London. I'm an Eastender, a West Ham fan. Transpired Fat Fred was a life-long Chelsea supporter. Football wise, no love lost!

Robredo bided his time so it didn't look like malice, but it came as no surprise when, after Edward Heath became Prime Minister, Waterman approached me one morning when I was a few minutes late, "Get your cards on Friday."

Just like that. No use of my name. A short, cold statement. When I had the temerity to ask why, he rattled off several reasons: poor timekeeping, insolence to a senior employee, refusing orders…

Didn't let the last one go, "National Service ended years ago. And I've never been insolent, Fat Fred."

My fellow workers gaped and gasped in disbelief.

Obviously, I received my cards before Friday.

To my surprise Vic Quigley sided with me. Not only as my shop steward. But also because he was a vehement opponent of both Waterman and Robredo.

"Let's take them on," Quigley advised. "We'll have the whole factory out: unfair dismissal. No one heard you say Fat Fred."

Thought about it. Seriously, I thought about what Quigley had said.

Looked him straight in the face. "Nah. Rather fight me own battles. In any case, why would I want to remain in this place? Robredo and Waterman will still be here."

Quigley laughed, placed a friendly hand on my shoulder, "You'll do all right, son. Believe me. You'll do all right."

* * *

Saturation: BBC1, BBC2, ITV, Channel Four, BBC News 24, Sky News.

Politicians of all colours competing in revolving door discussions, interviews and debates. All trotting out salient points, bullet points, from their probably expensively published manifestos. All promising to make our lives better.

Some of us have done all right. In spite of politicians. Some because of the existence of politicians. But not because of politicians.

Interesting quote from the famous communist Karl Marx: 'People make their own history, but not in conditions of their own making.'

About to switch off the television when the house phone rang.

House phone, you say. Well, it doesn't do to let every Tom, Dick and Harry have your mobile number. Know what I mean?

Millie handed me the phone. I listened to a recognisable voice, "Good evening Mr Slater. Andrew Marr, BBC Television."

Here it comes. Every blooming General Election since I retired.

Marr continued, "I wonder if, as a former leader, indeed General Secretary, of one of the UK's largest trade unions, you wish to comment on..."

*And in the naked light I saw*
*Ten thousand people, maybe more*
*People talking without speaking*
*People hearing without listening*
*People writing songs that voices never share*
*And no one dare*
*Disturb the sound of silence*

# HALFWAY TO PARADISE

The last place anybody of sound mind wanted to be was a rain sodden football ground in the north of England. Especially late October. One of those misty, cold nights when human breath cascaded into the chilliness: Boothferry Park, Hull.

This was where Eddie Rafferty, Third Division professional footballer, lay prostrate on a quagmire of a pitch in 1961, after being felled by a bone crunching tackle over the ball, dispensed by the stocky, opposing centre-half.

Play carried on for several minutes while a distraught Rafferty had to endure the catcalls, boos and jeers of the home crowd.

"Get up, you big Jessie" And: "There's nowt wrong wi' yo', Rafferty. On yer feet." And worse: comments of a cruder, Anglo-Saxon variety, calling the Irishman a ginger haired so an so.

Rafferty's team mates realised all was not well, surrounded the balding referee and urged him to allow the 'bucket and sponge' man onto the field to administer first aid. Choc Chilton, bucket and bag in hand, dashed across to the far touchline.

Choc, so called because of his love of all things chocolate, had been a successful goal scoring inside forward in the 1930s, but never had the nous to be a manager, or coach.

He leant over Eddie, examined his leg, which resulted in an excruciating, painful cry.

"For God's sake, Choc" in a harsher than usual Northern Irish accent.

"I'm no doctor, Eddie."

"You can bloody say that again."

Ignoring this now familiar remark Choc continued, "I'm no doctor, but this looks bad, Eddie. Very bad."

Rafferty seemed to be on the pitch for an eternity before St. John Ambulance arrived.

Just my rotten luck, he thought. On the verge of a transfer to one of the top clubs in The First Division. And this happens.

Always wanted to play in the big time. Always!

Creeping into his mind: the voice of his girlfriend Andrea's favourite singer: Billy Fury.

*I'm only halfway to paradise*
*So near, yet so far away*

Turned his head towards the main stand, from where the dark uniformed, peak-capped men hurried towards him carrying a stretcher.

"Don't want to end up a cripple," Rafferty said out loud.

"Nor will you be," retorted Choc.

"Andrea won't want to push me around in a bloody wheelchair."

*Bein' close to you is almost heaven*
*But seein' you can do just so much*

Rafferty tried, but failed, to stem the flow of tears. His teammates looked on with a mixture of sympathy and embarrassment. Noticeably, a couple of players were tearful themselves.

The two St. John's officers were not trained in the art of delicacy, nearly allowing the injured player to fall off the stretcher, effecting a sharp intake of rebuke.

"For Pete's sake. Who are you two, Laurel and Hardy?" exclaimed the injured footballer.

Mumbled apologies preceded the short journey to the dressing room, where a summoned doctor awaited Eddie Rafferty and various club officials, including the team manager Henry Browell; looked nothing like a football man, toffed up in a grey three piece suit.

Then again it was 1961: tracksuit managers were not in evidence. And the players had to take close season employment, usually manual labour, to make ends meet until the new season commenced.

For Eddie Rafferty, and hundreds of his contemporaries, playing football was for love of the game, coupled with an ambition to advance as far as possible, preferably to the dizzy heights of the First Division, winning titles and trophies along the way.

International recognition an added bonus of course.

However, Northern Ireland were never going to win the World Cup: Eddie was under no illusions about that. As for money, all he needed was enough for him and Andrea to live a comfortable life.

Much to his relief the doctor dispensed a pain-killing injection and let it take effect before carrying out a thorough examination of his left leg.

Left leg!

Rafferty's other thoughts and Billy Fury, had obliterated the obvious: his trusty left boot had dispatched nigh on seventy goals for his club since his debut as an eighteen-year-old in 1958.

Now?

Didn't bear thinking about.

The rain intensified, beat down on the roof of the ambulance, alarm ringing as it roared through the night, taking Eddie to the local Casualty Department.

Following day: a morose lower league footballer, left

leg encased in plaster, in hospital, in a strange town.

Eddie Rafferty stared out of the window of his room into the gloom, cut off from other patients. His manager believed he would enjoy some peace and quiet away from the questions of the Press.

Being Irish, Rafferty needed someone to talk to. Wasn't long before his wish was granted. Only it was not the kind of conversation he desired.

Choc Chilton, now suited and Henry Browell, both seeming uncomfortable, stood either side of the bed.

An awkward silence. The club officials' demeanour gave the game away.

"I'm not going to play again. Am I?"

Chilton looked to Browell. "You're better at this sort of stuff, Choc."

"For God's sake, Henry. You're the manager."

Rafferty cut in. "I'm sorry for your situation. It'd be nice to hear that for starters."

Browell wiped nervous sweat from his forehead and loosened his tie.

"Sorry, Eddie. We're both sorry. Let's wait for official medical opinion first."

Choc felt he had to add a comment of his own.

"It's a bummer, Eddie. If there was anything, is anything..."

Eddie didn't raise his voice, "Just go. Leave me. Need to think."

Chilton and Browell remained motionless, like a couple of lemons. Hard stare from Eddie prompted them to exit the room.

Browell first. But as Chilton neared the threshold, The young ex-player spoke, "What's the problem Choc? My injury. What is it?"

"Anterior cruciate ligament. In your knee. Shattered."

"Will I walk? Eventually?"

"Yes. But you'll never play football again. Sorry."

A sheepish Choc Chilton left the lad from Belfast to his own devices: thoughts, nightmares. Call them what you will.

Glad he held it together when the two men were present. But now, by himself, realisation setting in, Eddie Rafferty quietly sobbed.

* * *

The clock's ticking: only two minutes remaining of the 1962 FA Cup Final. Couldn't put a paper between the competing teams: defences on top, for sure.

Hang on a sec: Delaney's lost the ball on the halfway line, could be a break on.

United's Nicky Stephens making a strong run on the right wing, with inside left Eddie Rafferty indicating he wants the ball. He's found space for himself.

Stephens easily beats a couple of retreating defenders, crosses the ball towards Rafferty.

Can he reach it? It's high.

The inside left chests down the ball and, as it drops, volleys goalwards.

It's in! A goal! A brilliant goal!

Rafferty's mobbed by his team mates as the referee puts his whistle to his lips: game over. And young Eddie Rafferty, in his first ever Cup Final has won it for United with the last kick of the match.

"Yeah, we've done it. Fantastic, Eee-aye-adio, we've won the cup."

The hard bitten Matron looked down at Eddie sprawled out on the floor of his hospital room.

"Mr Rafferty, what on earth are you doing?"

Grinning, he peered up at Matron. "I scored. Scored the winner."

Staff Nurse Marcie O'Brien poked her head into the

room, looked kindly at Eddie.

"Won the Cup for United, Marcie."

Ignoring her superior, she helped the confused footballer back into his bed, displacing her hat off her auburn bob.

"You've been having another of your dreams, Eddie," Marcie said softly in her Southern Irish brogue.

"No dream. I did it. Scored the..."

His words trailed away.

Marcie sat on the edge of his bed, comforting the broken ex- footballer .

Eddie's tears spilled out onto her starched uniform.

Before departing, Matron reprimanded the two youngsters. "Staff Nurse O'Brien, Mr Rafferty. Show some decorum."

* * *

Andrea took her time. Nearly a week had elapsed since Eddie's hospitalisation.

He was non-too pleased. Okay, she couldn't drive. And she was seventy miles away. But… he wasn't at Land's End.

Unfortunately for Rafferty her visit coincided with one of Staff Nurse O'Brien's duties.

A chance for jovial banter.

Andrea, a petite blonde, stood in the doorway, face set rigid.

Marcie guessed who it was and, with her almond eyes casting a sideways glance, made herself scarce.

Rafferty's girlfriend was intrigued about "this affection you have."

He told her the Staff Nurse cheered him up.

An argument ensued, Eddie wanting to know why Andrea had never put in an earlier appearance.

"I have to work, Eddie."

"Could've telephoned. Anyway, you work for your father."

He grimaced, me and my mouth. Ever since meeting Andrea, she'd been badgering him to take an active interest in John Varney Associates, a legal firm founded by her father. But Eddie was a football man, in whatever capacity, as he informed his girlfriend on numerous occasions.

"You're better than that, Eddie. Wouldn't have to labour on building sites every summer."

In that instance, Rafferty's career in tatters, Andrea let the matter rest. Instead, the couple exchanged pleasantries about nothing in particular: the weather, Christmas, hospital food, all interspersed with periods of awkward silence.

The bell rang: time to go. The briefest of kisses from Andrea. End of visit.

His room door left open. At his request. Liked to see people pass by. Some patients now knew the "Irish Wonder" was in their midst. And that his football career was finished.

Accepted it now: well, up to a point. Wanted to recover as best as he could. Then see what was on offer. In the game. Working in an office for Andrea's father was NOT an option. Where that would leave his relationship with her?

Rafferty drifted off into a deep sleep, trying not to think, or dream, of football.

* * *

Eddie Rafferty's rehabilitation had been slow. Christmas came and went. 1962 arrived to the strains of Acker Bilk's clarinet playing "Stranger On The Shore".

Back in his parents' home on the North Yorkshire's east coast he had to contend with Andrea's regular visits, which amounted to her vigorous recruiting campaign on behalf of John Varney.

A winter of discontent.

An improvement in the weather greeted March and saw Eddie head for the town centre after his final physiotherapy session. Then a meeting with Choc Chilton. This took place in a cafe as neither of them were big drinkers of alcohol.

"Has Henry Browell sent you, Choc?"

Silence.

"Okay, spit it out. What's the deal?"

Chilton shuffled uncomfortably in his seat.

"I pleaded on your behalf, Eddie. Believe me."

Snorting laugh from Eddie.

After the derisory offer of a one-off payment of £500, he asked Choc Chilton to leave.

A young, dyed blonde waitress, clearing tables. "Cheer up, love, it may never happen."

"Already has," Rafferty exclaimed.

As she picked up Chilton's cup and saucer he looked her straight in the eye.

"I could've played for United. My club would've got thirty thousand for me."

Sardonic smile from the waitress. "If you say so, love."

She trotted off through to the kitchen. Rafferty mused over what might have been while music played on the jukebox. Maybe Andrea was right: cannot spend the rest of my life doing nothing.

Frankie Vaughan's voice filled the cafe.

*If I were a tower of strength, I'd walk away*
*I'd look in your eyes and here's what I'd say*
*I don't want you, I don't need you*
*I don't love you anymore*
*And I'd walk out the door*

# THE RIVER OF DREAMS

1977: Abba riding high in the charts.

*Money, money, money*
*Must be funny*
*In the rich man's world*
*Money, money, money*
*Always sunny*
*It's a rich man's world*

"Come on, Eddie, let's have the skip on the bus. It IS the away kit?"

"Orange shirts?" enquired Eddie, kitman of the Los Angeles Aztecs.

"Yes," responded coach Christie.

Eddie knew the shirts were orange. Just winding him up. As the skip, containing the American soccer club's kit and boots were loaded onto the bus, Eddie Rafferty, as he always did when leaving for an away game, took in the view: the high, slim, white concrete arch (leading to the Aztec's home ground) emblazoned with the legend – LOS ANGELES MEMORIAL COLISEUM.

Under this were the five Olympic Rings.

He'd already sat in the Californian sunshine inside the 92,000 capacity stadium, in front of the Executive Suites, taking in a contemplative, panoramic vista of the skyscrapers beyond. A ten-minute ritual Rafferty never tired of.

An hour later he was up in the air bound for the Big Apple, where the LA Aztecs would play New York Cosmos, a team which featured the great Brazilian footballer: Pele.

Still, the Aztecs boasted their own superstar: George Best.

As Eddie relaxed back in his seat, the man himself walked by, glass of white wine in hand. As usual, Bestie smiled at him: a man of few words. Still…

Rain greeted the Aztec's entourage outside Kennedy Airport, where they waited for transport to their hotel. Briefly, Rafferty's mind drifted back to the fateful October night in 1961. He pinched himself.

Once settled in his hotel room, Eddie Rafferty picked up his bedside telephone, dialled his home in LA. On away trips, at this juncture, he always phoned his wife. And he knew, with a great degree of certainty, that Marcie would pick up within five rings.

# DON'T LOOK BACK IN ANGER

Davy McIntyre had lost everything to pursue his dream: secure job (more of a career really), comfortable homes, wife and son.

*Sweet dream baby*
*How long must I dream*
*Dream baby got me dreaming sweet dreams*
*The whole day through*
*Dream baby got me dreaming sweet dreams*
*Night time too*

1972: fifteen-year-old Davy, wearing his white-blonde hair long, hunched over his white electric guitar (white being the football strip colour of his beloved Leeds United), hammering out the throbbing riff of Brown Sugar, a hit for The Rolling Stones the previous year.

Early evening in his local youth club, with only a handful of youngsters, plus club leader Tommy Gardener in attendance. He glanced over his shoulder, nodded.

Out of the shadow of a doorway a dread-locked West Indian man approached Tommy and stood alongside him. Both men witnessed an impromptu performance of intensive virtuosity.

Davy was oblivious to his audience, continuing for another couple of minutes.

Tommy and club members had seen it all many

times, just smiled in appreciation.

The West Indian, tall and in his late twenties applauded loudly. In surprise, Davy looked up. His club leader and newcomer moved briskly towards him.

Introductions: Dreadlocks christened Disraeli Kanhai.

The young guitarist tentatively shook his hand. Kanhai went on to explain that he was lead singer with the heavy metal group, Introspective. They had been getting by for a short while with bass and rhythm guitars, plus drums.

"Lead guitar? enquired Davy.

"That's where you come in, man," replied Kanhai in a diluted West Midlands accent.

Even though Introspective had not yet signed a record deal, young McIntyre felt he had no option but to take up Disraeli Kanhai's offer.

Pauline McIntyre, barely out of school, had tried her best in difficult circumstances: useless, older husband cleared off back to Glasgow after less than a year of marriage, leaving her heavily pregnant, living in a Victorian slum in Hunslet, a suburban area of Leeds.

By the time Procol Harum topped the music charts with "A Whiter Shade Of Pale" in 1967,Pauline and her ten-year-old son Davy had relocated, courtesy of Leeds City Council, to the notorious Quarry Hill Flats. Though for Pauline, her fifth floor, two-bed property was an improvement on the 'back to back' in which she existed.

The balcony was a novelty; bathroom, toilet and ventilated larder luxuries.

However, the envisaged 'model community was beset with social problems and vandalism during the late 1960s, exacerbating Pauline's despair.

Davy was left to fend for himself when she descended into alcoholism, resulting in his mother's death at an early age.

His one salvation was an ability to teach himself to master the guitar. To start with an acoustic model his father had left under the stairs at their home in Hunslet. Davy convinced himself McIntyre Senior left the guitar behind by way of a present, a consolation for abandoning wife and child. Pauline told her son his father could strum the instrument. No more than that. Davy felt it WAS more than that, he felt he'd inherited a gift to play 'by ear'.

It was a gift, which drove Pauline to distraction sometimes, particularly when she was suffering from an horrendous hangover, venting her anger and frustration on her son, causing Tommy Gardener much concern. Not believing for one second facial cuts and bruises were the result of Davy walking into doors, tripping on uneven paths or whatever.

He understood the lad's loyalty to his mother, but took him under his wing on Davy's thirteenth birthday, keeping a watchful eye at the youth club, where he allowed him to assist with maintenance, for which he was paid. Tommy encouraged Davy to save up enough to buy an electric guitar.

Kanhai had witnessed true talent and berated himself for apprehensively regarding Tommy's narrative as a 'sob story'.

As the 1970s progressed, Davy felt it was only a matter of time before Introspective emulated their heroes: Deep Purple and Black Sabbath.

Although Disraeli founded Introspective and managed to secure sufficient engagements (clubs, pubs, weddings) to enable all five members to enjoy more than a reasonable standard of living, a lingering clash of personalities between him and rebellious drummer, Jordan Garner, threatened to split the group.

This conflict unsettled Davy.

After all, he'd joined Introspective to bring some kind of balance to his life.

Then, in 1974, a lucky break. The group had a gig at a Liverpool backstreet pub: as rough as.

By chance, a London record producer with time to kill, dropped into the establishment on hearing live music.

Introspective were his 'bag'.

A now confident Davy was under the impression the deal clincher was his guitar work.

In the recording studio, the producer, Maxwell Thorngumbald, left all group members under no illusions it was Disraeli's finely judged, but raucous inflection which landed them a recording contract, albeit a short term one. Until they 'proved themselves'.

Davy was miffed, to say the least, still carrying a working class chip on his shoulder. However, he still got on reasonably well with his benefactor. Even though he was several rungs up the social class ladder, having a public school/Oxbridge background.

It was this background which enabled Disraeli Kanhai to establish a firm friendship with Thorngumbald, who had been similarly educated and thought of himself sharing the same plateau as George Martin, The Beatles record producer.

Appearance wise, Thorngumbald was a diminutive, lank haired scruff, with an unfortunate pock marked face, lending credence to the stories of him being shifty.

The man was full of himself. Acted without thinking. And Davy was often hurt by his pointed, class ridden gibes. Disraeli, on the other hand was a modest, caring sort of guy and informed the sensitive guitarist it would benefit his state of mind If he remained oblivious to Thorngumbald's crass behaviour. This course of action, the West Indian added, would irritate the producer no end – "Trust me. It will."

Affinity between the pair had kept Davy on the straight and narrow in an industry well known for its excesses.

But…

Disraeli was extremely ambitious. Allowed nothing, including drugs and booze, to inhibit his aspirations.

Told Davy on more than one occasion he could join the ride to the top, that Jordan Garner would drag them all down; Disraeli was having none of that. Never wavered from his stance.

Even when three consecutive Number Ones came Introspective's way.

Indeed this was a platform from which Kanhai would spring into a solo career, leaving an indecisive Davy floundering in a heavy metal band (group no longer de rigeur) which under-appreciated his undoubted talent.

Not that Introspective as a whole floundered.

They hooked into a record buying public whose tastes had switched from singles to albums.

The band duly delivered two massive selling long playing records. On both sides of the Atlantic. And without Kanhai, who had, by the end of the Seventies, carved out a lucrative profession as a solo singer in Los Angeles. His leading role in Introspective had been taken by Jordan Garner, who'd always fancied himself as the next Phil Collins.

Davy had always thought of himself as a working musician. But like thousands before him, became seduced by the adulation, particularly of the younger females in their audiences.

As 1979 faded away, the still young McIntyre smiled to himself as he listened to the Pretenders singing "Brass in Pocket" summed up his life perfectly.

After an open air gig in Dusseldorf, Davy met the girl who was to become his wife: Steffi Dortmunder, who, because of her Swedish mother, inherited her typically blonde Scandinavian looks.

Steffi was five years older than the youthful lead guitarist of Introspective. A go-getter with wealthy parents. Mother a leading economist in the German finance industry, father a prominent lawyer in Munich: a combination of talents which would be to the detriment of Davy McIntyre's well being, both materially and mentally.

Steffi's control of her husband mimicked that of Yoko Ono's over John Lennon. And his fellow band members didn't like it at all.

By now Jordan Garner was marketing Introspective big time, involving all kinds of unsavoury characters. This irritated Steffi to such an extent she suggested her father became the band's manager as his legal know-how would eradicate any pitfalls and dispense with the coterie of spongers, hangers-on and con men.

A clash of personalities was inevitable. Garner accused her of interfering and Davy of being unable to control his wife.

Steffi's next tack was to propose her father being hired as a consultant: no deal.

She was caught between the easy going Davy and vociferous Garner, trying to please them both. And failing.

Situation worsening when the drummer was addressed by Steffi as 'Garner'. He retaliated by referring to her as 'Dortmunder'.

In private she continually urged Davy to split from the band to pursue a solo career.

"A musical split means no money splits," she advised her husband.

As a youngster he was surrounded by poverty: the opposite applied as the 1980s progressed.

Steffi's childhood, however, was immersed in

opulence, wanted for nothing: spoilt rotten.

Wealth, therefore, was not the attraction when making a play for Davy McIntyre. No, it was the glamour. Being noticed, photographed, featuring on magazine covers.

All about Steffi Dortmunder: never used her married name. Being, in fact, an additional member of Introspective.

Having said that, Steffi preferred to spend her husband's money, rather than her own inherited wealth: homes in New York, Paris and London.

Motors more for show than driving: Porsche, Bugatti, Mercedes, Bentley. And a Roller of course.

Fashion houses welcomed her.

Davy took his eye off the ball. Even more so when his son Marcus was born on 13th July 1985: Live Aid.

Davy McIntyre was over the proverbial moon.

Steffi was peed off: she wanted a seat at Wembley Stadium as near as possible to Princess Diana to witness the "gig of the century".

As Steffi explained, "A massive photo opportunity missed."

"You've given your own performance of a lifetime" Davy told her, slight annoyance in his voice, "And my son will have a father when he's growing up."

Famous last words.

Well, not quite: 1987, a game changer.

When Davy listened to the Number One single of March that year: Stand By Me, by Ben E.King, little did he realise, that weeks later, King's maudlin refrain would haunt him for quite some time after Steffi and Marcus disappeared from McIntyre's life.

Not only had she taken his son, but manipulated his finances in her favour to such an extent, that he was left on the verge of bankruptcy. He was left, however, with enough money to hire a private investigator who tracked down Steffi: living in a Bavarian fortress under the vigilant protection of her now powerful father. Further enquiries were terminated by an intimidating, shaven headed security officer brandishing a firearm.

Game changer? Game over!

Davy McIntyre fell into a deep depression. But resisted all alcohol and drug related remedies. Even though fellow band members, lead by Jordan Garner, felt it was cool to pursue this well trodden path. Consequently, Introspective's music became more and more bizarre, leading to a drastic reduction in popularity.

The Nineties saw the rise of the Indie sound. Introspective trailed in its wake. And although Davy recovered his financial status, when the hits dried up he left the band. His attempts at pursuing a solo career bombed: his association with Introspective tainted.

The Millennium: Davy McIntyre working as a postman in Leeds. He'd had enough of the fame, for sure. Not the fortune, though. Well, up to a point. Didn't want to return to his younger years of struggle. Needed enough of a cash flow however to get by comfortably. Being a postman was the day job. By night he was gigging in down at heel pubs.

Five years later Davy found himself homeless, jobless and desperate for a change when his on-off relationship with barmaid Hattie crumbled because of his depression.

"Take a long hard look in the mirror and change what you see," she told him.

Even he had to admit that he now had the appearance of someone approaching sixty rather than fifty. Physically, he'd not looked after himself: no regular exercise, combined with bingeing on junk food. Only saving grace: no alcohol, no drugs.

His once white blonde hair more grey, worn in a shorter style.

A recent, and rare, pub gig had been attended by an old Introspective fan, sad to see the decline of Davy McIntyre, who implored him not to let on to the Press.

Luckily for Davy, the fan not only had no desire to blab to the papers, but was the owner of a popular gymnasium in Harrogate.

The former lead guitarist studied the proffered business card:

**Jim's Gym**

Proprieter: James Banks-Sutton

Dumbells, kettleballs and multi-press racks. Davy's entry into the world of fitness. Lengths of breaststroke in the pool increasing daily.

Two weeks in: fit enough to tackle bench presses, power cages.

His final week: cross trainer, exercise bike, treadmill.

Showering off the sweat, Davy dressed in a clean white shirt paired with black Wranglers and returned Banks-Sutton's favour: played his white guitar and sang at the wedding reception of Virginia Banks-Sutton and her groom.

Father looked on in admiration, as much for Davy McIntyre as for his daughter.

Healthier, fitter, grey hair formed into an early Presley style, a rejuvenated Davy, belying his fifty plus years, treated his attentive audience to a selection of songs loved by his late mother: late Fifties, early Sixties, featuring Eddie Cochran, Buddy Holly and Bobby Vee.

Something for everyone: raucous 'C'mon Everybody', gentle 'Everyday', and rousing 'The Night Has A Thousand Eyes'.

But the renewal of the former lead guitarist of

Introspective ended with his tender rendition of an Oasis classic:

*Slip inside the eye of your mind*
*Don't you know you might find*
*A better place to play*
*You said that you'd never been*
*All the things that you've seen*
*Will slowly fade away*
*Don't look back in anger*
*I heard you say*

Born again Davy McIntyre, carrying his guitar, climbed down the steps of a Jet2 aircraft into the humidity of a Majorcan June evening.

Made his way through Palma Airport to carousel number nineteen to retrieve his distinctive purple suitcase.

Waiting for the hotel transfer coach he caught sight of his reflection in a full length window: lean, toned body, attired in black jeans and white shirt, sunglasses dangling from a belt loop.

Only acknowledgement to his heavy metal past: greying hair tied back in a ponytail. Some things not easy to change. Though the metal framed specs were new.

As he travelled northwards from Majorca's capital, he gazed at his one-way airline ticket, his face creasing into a satisfying smile: no turning back now.

He hated the phrase "The first day of the rest of my life".

But to McIntyre it was.

He was the last passenger to be dropped off, Sergio, the driver, having to wake him up.

Davy felt good about himself and, wanting to share his good fortune, pressed a 10 Euro note into the

Spaniard's hand.

Sergio's response surprised him, "No, Senor. I work. I am paid. But I thank you. Gracias."

Reluctantly, the Englishman re-pocketed the money, but was happy to shake the extended hand.

As Sergio climbed back into the driver's seat, after reacquainting Davy with his case and guitar, he sang the opening verse of Introspective's first Number One, looked down at the guitarist and smiled.

"Adios, Senor McIntyre. Beuna suerte."

The coach's electric door closed, leaving a nonplussed Davy McIntyre standing at the rear of his hotel in Puerto Pollensa. Nonplussed because prior to departing the UK, James Banks-Sutton, in further gratitude for performing at his daughter's wedding, arranged for Davy a passport in the name of Bjorn Henriksson, Swedish session musician.

His knowledge of the Spanish language was limited, but he knew the meaning of 'Buena suerte.'

Good luck. He'd need it.

Already decided his first fortnight would be one of total relaxation, including plenty of swimming in the calm Mediterranean, a hundred yards from his hotel.

Kept himself to himself. Hoping no Introspective fans were staying, or even worse, living on the island.

Drew comfort from the fact that his current appearance was a radical change from his previous life.

Davy loved the classy hotel. But long term it would be very expensive.

Thinking out loud: another two weeks before sounding out low-key bars, which would provide accommodation in return for musical entertainment.

Didn't want any old bar. Or dive. However, beggars can't...

Following just over a week of visits, he found what

he was looking for: friendly bar run by a Majorcan family – two grown-ups around the sixty mark, son late thirties, his slightly older sister.

Davy introduced himself as Bjorn to Pablo, wife Monica and their offspring Jordi and Sophia, whom he took a particular shine to, likening her to Spanish actress Penelope Cruz.

Davy's accommodation above the bar was basic. But at least he had a sea view.

He tried to affect something of a Swedish accent, not too over the top. God help him if any Swedes entered Pablo's Bar: bridge too far to cross?

Davy's repertoire: mainly Dylan, Holly, Eddie Cochran. Open to requests. Definitely no Introspective though!

He sat on a barstool close to the bar's entrance, affording him views of the marina, the exterior heat tempered by air conditioning.

Audiences were appreciative.

Alcohol offerings from satisfied customers always refused – politely!

A contented summer for Davy. Only one moment of consternation: a request for an Introspective number – courteously declined on the grounds of ignorance.

The winter was an eye opener for Davy: a fall off in temperature. And rain!

Still... Pablo's was very popular with locals, Bjorn Henriksson being a star draw.

2007: Davy's fiftieth birthday.

As early summer approached, Puerto Pollensa was greeting tourists once again, new and long standing. In no small measure as far as Pablo was concerned, due to the laid back vocals and guitar playing of Bjorn

Henriksson.

Bonus for all fans in '07: Sophia joined Bjorn on several songs. In particular, Tell Me How (Holly number). Sitting In The Balcony (Cochran) and I Threw It All Away (Dylan).

Life couldn't get any better than this; this lovely uncomplicated life.

*Sweet dream baby*
*How long...*

One burning night in July, Sophia joined Bjorn at the bar, both drinking long iced Cokes.

"We seem to have a regular admirer," she said. "Or should I say: you do."

"Really? Where is she?"

"Not a she. A he."

"C'mon, Sophia, I'm not..."

"I know that for a fact. Still, seems to be taking an interest."

Sweat on his brow. Not what he wanted.

POLICE? IMMIGRATION? Or? Someone from his past, someone who recognised him.

God, I'm being introspective, thought Davy.

Sophia discreetly pointed out this interloper: tallish, mid-forties, short dark hair, square jawed features, with the world-weary appearance of... a policeman.

His initial thoughts were right.

Even more worrying, Sophia had seen him on several occasions during the past three or four weeks.

Davy completed his third set of the night around eleven-thirty. Sophia, by then, was helping out behind the still busy bar. He indicated to her he was going out for a stroll.

The inquisitive stranger was nowhere to be seen. Despite the hour, it was nevertheless, overpoweringly

Puerto Pollensa, Majorca

hot, so he headed for the marina with hopes of cooler air. Some hope.

From his bench seat Davy took in the panoramic view ahead of the famous Pine Walk winding its way around to the Hotel Illa D'or and beyond, restaurant and bar lights contrasting against the midnight blue sky.

Focus on the here and now, he kept telling himself.

But... remnants of his past life kept creeping into his mind.

*Slip inside the eye of your mind...*

McIntyre was jolted out of his reverie from behind by a gentle hand on his shoulder. He knew who it was before turning his head.

"Beautiful view."

"Yes. It is," responded Davy. "Even better in daylight."

Then, facing the stranger from Pablo's bar, "But you'll have seen it many times."

The stranger sat down. Close up he appeared even more weary. Couldn't hold Davy's stare though, speaking as he looked down at the ground, "Marcus wants to see you."

This matter of fact statement took McIntyre completely by surprise inwardly, but outwardly he remained calm. "Think you've got the wrong guy."

His companion now faced Davy. "Pablo's advertise you as Bjorn Henriksson. But I know you're Davy McIntyre," he said in a recognisable American accent.

Composed response, "Sure about that?"

"One hundred per cent. Got your DNA off a Coke bottle a couple of weeks back."

"Who the hell are you?"

Outstretched right hand, refused. "Lewis Rayner, private investigator."

Davy listened intently as Rayner detailed his assignment: hired by Marcus to seek out his father. Steffi had never been maternal. Aged ten, Marcus sent to live with her divorced sister in LA.

Davy remembered Steffi's sibling. Met her, in fact. When Introspective toured the States.

Petra. Petra Kruetzman. Made a play for Davy. She was a bit part actress with designs on forcing her way into the music industry. Only her voice never matched her looks. And when Davy was wavering, Jordan Garner bluntly told her to stick to acting.

Looking back, Garner saved Davy a hell of a lot of grief.

His reminisces had blocked out Rayner, mind in overdrive.

The future: Davy, Petra and Marcus playing happy families. Visits from Steffi. Her father even. Marcus getting into the music business. Father and son reforming Introspective. Into the limelight once more.

"Are you getting all this, McIntyre? Need to get back to Marcus."

Davy stood up, looked down at Rayner.

"How much money do you want? How much for you to say you couldn't track me down?"

# THE MASTERPLAN

It was a rush. Too much of a rush. Cissy, aged 76, Jimmy nearly 80. Glad our case has wheels, he thought. Bet Jimmy's glad I splashed out on a Simonite case, thought Cissy. With wheels.

With a minute to spare the couple were side by side in their reserved seats on the Hull to London Kings Cross train.

"Nearly didn't make it," Jimmy gasps.

"We did make it. So stop moaning," his wife retorted.

Jimmy stands, takes off his grey jacket, straightens his green patterned tie and settles into his seat. Fussily, he attempts to hand rub creases out of his white shirt.

He is disconcerted by Cissy's stare.

"Now what's up?" he says.

"Apart from your continual faffing?"

No answer.

"I said it at the time and I'm saying it again – your hair."

"What's wrong with it?" was Jimmy's hurt reply.

"You looked perfectly fine with grey hair. Dying it black... well, you look... ridiculous."

"People say I look twenty years younger. Anyway, I like it."

"People are lying to you, Jimmy."

She pauses. "It was that film. Wasn't it?"

"What film?"

"The old black and white one with a young, VERY

YOUNG, Cary Grant. We watched it a few weeks ago. And even he didn't dye his hair when he became older."

"Hello."

An interruption to their conversation by a polite, young man of mixed race. The youngster smiles at Jimmy and Cissy as he lodges a pear shaped, black case in the luggage rack. The smile is followed by an appraisal of his fellow passengers: the bloke had obviously coloured his hair, but had a kindly face. And his partner, although advancing in years, was smartly dressed, but not ridiculously youthful in her choice of clothes, her pleasant face framed by mid length, silver hair cut in layers.

The young man's elder brother was a hairdresser, who'd experimented on family and friends during his training, hence a fascination with hair, which he thought told a lot about a person's character.

"What's that in your case – a machine gun?" Jimmy says out of the blue.

A laugh from the youngster. "My violin."

Cissy glowers at Jimmy. "You'll have to excuse my husband. He comes out with the daftest things."

"You wouldn't believe the number of people who ask me the same question. I'm Alfie by the way," his accent refined, no local trace.

"Cissy. This is Jimmy."

"Pleased to meet you both."

Jimmy genuine with his response. "Pleased to meet you, lad."

He studied this casually, but smartly dressed young gentleman sitting directly opposite. Reminded the older man of someone. Racked his brain. Thoughts interrupted by Cissy.

"Get our tickets out, Jimmy. The guard's on his way."

"Bodyguard!" Jimmy blurted out, causing

passengers round about to stare.

"What the heck are you on about?" his exasperated wife utters.

"The young lad here – Alfie. Don't mind if I call you Alfie do you?"

Turned to Cissy. "Bodyguard. That thing we watch Sunday nights."

"Get to the point."

"Alfie here. He's the spitting image of the bloke who plays the bodyguard. Younger version mind you. And the telly one's not as suntanned."

"The guy who plays the bodyguard" she says, in a correcting sort of way. "No one says bloke these days. Isn't that right, Alfie?"

Jimmy gives Alfie no time to answer. "Yes, well, the actor who plays him could be Alfie's father."

"Hardly," responds Cissy, "Richard Madden's not that old."

"Richard Madden? Who's Richard Madden?"

"Keep up, Jimmy."

Looking up from his smartphone, Alfie cuts in,"He's the actor who plays David Budd, the bodyguard. I'm only nineteen, so couldn't be my father. Brother maybe?"

Cissy regards her husband with an air of superiority. "That's told you, mister."

Alfie smiles. Cissy folds her arms. Jimmy, non-plussed, gazes out of the window.

A period of silence.

Jimmy soon tires of window gazing, engages his young companion in conversation.

Alfie reveals he began playing the violin aged seven and gradually progressed, via tuition, to a high standard: regular performances in his school orchestras and Sixth Form College, leading to Alfie freelancing and playing his favourite musical instrument at various events, mainly in the north of England. Latterly, at his old school Hymers College in Hull. Currently studying at the London College of Music.

"So after your degree you'll be getting a job in music?" enquires Jimmy.

Not looking up from a book she is reading, Cissy remarks, "No, he'll be getting a job as a window cleaner."

"What?" says her perplexed husband.

"Why do you think the lad's attending a college of music?"

Trying to diffuse the situation, Alfie addresses Jimmy. "What do you do for a living, if you don't mind my asking?"

"He was a window cleaner," says Cissy.

"Not all my life, Cissy. Be fair. Alfie'll be under the impression I'm a right dunderhead."

"You don't say," said Cissy sarcastically.

Jimmy ignores this remark and put some spin on his world of work, which started aged fifteen, in the early 1950s: general stores administrator, logistics facilitator and twenty years working as a public servant.

"I'm impressed," says Alfie.

Cissy's eyes still fixed on her book, but commenting nevertheless, "Aye, well don't be. To give those occupations their proper titles, they were: stock clerk, glorified errand lad and public servant is a rather fancy label for a Council binman."

She looks up."His first two jobs lasted five minutes. And the golden handshake from the Council allowed him to be a self employed window cleaner for the rest of his working life."

An awkward period of quiet.

Jimmy is crestfallen.

Alfie feels Cissy's comments are harsh. But then again, he didn't know how their lives had panned out.

As his Sixth Form College politics lecturer said to him once,"Don't be judgemental."

It was Alfie who fractured the silence, addressing the couple together, "Journey's end London?"

"Yes, lad," replies Jimmy "For the tennis."

Alfie's face lights up with interest. "The ATP Finals at the O2 Arena?"

"That's right," answers Cissy. "Been a good year. Wimbledon in the summer. Now this."

"Icing on the cake," states Jimmy. "Tennis your thing, Alfie?"

"Definitely. Play when I can. And last year holidayed with my family near Manacou. Where Rafa Nadal lives."

"See him at all?" enquires Jimmy.

"Don't be daft, Jimmy. He will have been playing tennis," uttered Cissy.

"Depends when Alfie went to Majorca."

Alfie decided not to become involved. He plugged earphones into his smartphone, content to relax with some music.

Cissy's reading continues. As the rain sodden, lush green countryside flashes by his window, Jimmy nods off. The train rumbles on at a steady pace.

Then: a jolt. This serves to dislodge a sleeping Alfie's earphones and awaken Jimmy.

His curiosity gets the better of him.

After a short while listening through the earphones, he held them close to his wife so she could share the music :

*Take the time to make some sense*
*Of what you want to say*
*And cast your words away upon the waves*
*Sail them home with acquiesce*

"Give them back to the lad," Cissy utters.

Jimmy does as he's told. "Doesn't sound very classical to me."

Glowers at her husband. "I hope you took note of the opening lines."

"Pardon?"

"Take the time to make some sense of what you want to say."

"Very funny."

Alfie awakes, sees his earphones on the table. "Hope the music didn't disturb you both."

"No, not at all," replies Jimmy after reciting some of the lyrics of Masterplan. "It wasn't classical. Was it?"

Alfie goes on to tell Jimmy about his wide musical tastes, from Sinatra to Buddy Holly, The Beatles, Michael Buble, jazz greats like Miles Davis and Thelonious Monk.

"But classical is my thing. Vivaldi in particular. The Four Seasons is fantastic."

"You can say that again," remarks Jimmy, "Had some great hits: Walk Like a Man, Big Girls Don't Cry, December...

Cissy swiftly interjects. "Not those Four Seasons, you clot."

Alfie kindly puts the older man right, explaining that the Italian composer Antonio Vivaldi's Four Seasons was a group of four violin concertos, giving musical expression to the seasons of the year.

"Oh, I see," says Jimmy meekly, scowling at his wife.

Still concentrating on her book Cissy can't resist ending the topic, "I think the penny's dropped."

Changing the subject. This is Alfie's way of diffusing the enmity. "You both mentioned you'd been to Wimbledon this year. How did you manage to get hold of tickets?"

Cissy steps in to brief the youngster, feeling her

husband has dominated most of the conversation. Alfie is interested to know about the Wimbledon ticket ballot. Now he's well informed, will definitely enter the ballot for the following year's Championships.

"Don't get your hopes up though, Alfie. It was four years before we got a sniff of tickets," explained Cissy.

"Then it was only Number Three Court," retorts Jimmy.

"Trust you to put a damper on things," says his wife.

"It was you who said it took years."

"I didn't want to raise the lad's hopes. That's all."

"Well, you certainly didn't do that."

"Look, Jimmy...

An embarrassed Alfie stands up. "If you'll excuse me. Need the toilet."

He makes his way down the aisle, away from the quarrelling couple.

Cissy faces Jimmy. They are practically nose to nose.

"Now look what you've gone and done," an annoyed Cissy said.

"Me?"

"Yes. You."

"Cissy, I'm not..."

A gruff Scottish voice from behind."When you two dobbers've finished, there are people here who want a bit o' peace and quiet."

Jimmy stands, turns to see a rather well built, ginger bearded, scar-faced, middle-aged man. Despite Cissy grabbing hold of her husband's arm, an attempt to prevent Jimmy from becoming involved in a potentially nasty situation, he soldiers on.

"What did you call us, you Scotch git?"

The Scotsman stands up. "You heard me. Bampots an' all if you ask me."

Jimmy was familiar with the Scottish vernacular, having been billeted with Glaswegians in the army during his National Service. Both men leave their seats and end up face to face.

Cissy is concerned.

Even more so when Jimmy responds with, "You are a bawface. And a doaty to boot."

Alfie is returning from the toilet and has witnessed some of the altercation; could see that Jimmy is about to be clattered by the irate Scot. The youngster pushes his way past standing passengers, as the Jock is on the point of exploding, his contorted face becoming redder and redder, right hand pulled back preparing to deliver a blow, with the elderly man's fragile face the target.

To the surprise of many, Jimmy in particular, Alfie wards off the Scotsman's right hand with his own left and digs a right hand index finger into the temple, rendering the assailant immobile.

Alfie then forces the two men to apologise to each other and shake hands.

An air of calm descends inside the rail carriage. Admiring glances filter in the direction of the hero of the hour. Jimmy becomes fidgety, glances sideways at his wife.

More to himself than anyone else, he mutters, "Another second and that Scotsman was dead meat. You don't forget your army training."

Cissy, who appeared to be snoozing, elbows Jimmy hard.

He responds. "Only saying."

"Well don't," she says, eyes firmly shut,"you should be thanking Alfie for saving your bacon"

"I did. Didn't I, son? And I thank you once more. I really do."

Alfie merely smiles, goes back to listening to something on his smartphone.

* * *

"Your next stop is Grantham. Grantham is your next stop. Please ensure you have all your belongings with you when you leave the train."

This sudden announcement shakes Jimmy out of his reverie. Cissy still reading. Alfie checks his watch while studying passengers milling around the platform before spying a discarded Guardian newspaper on the table across the aisle. He pulls it over, spreads it out in front of himself.

"Bit of highbrow reading there, lad. Still, someone of your education wouldn't settle for anything less," comments Jimmy. "Unless it's The Times of course. I'm an Express man myself."

Alfie smiles. "Actually, it's the sport I prefer in The Guardian. Have you ever read Paul MacInnes?"

"I've drunk Guinness. Never heard of MacInnes" replies Jimmy, laughing at his own feeble attempt at humour.

Smiling weakly, Alfie continues "He did a good piece on Tottenham Hotspur recently.

Their new stadium not quite ready, so still playing at Wembley."

"You're a fan?"

"My girlfriend is. She's converted me."

"My own career was cut short. A leg break."

"You were a pro?"

"Well, scouts were impressed."

Cissy, alert as ever, cuts in, "No, he wasn't a pro, Alfie. When he mentions scouts, he means Boy Scouts.He played football for them. Always reckoned his Scoutmaster brought him to the attention of Leeds United. As for his broken leg, his mother told me he did that walking backwards on a wall."

A puzzled Alfie. "Why would he do that?"

"Why indeed?" exclaimed Cissy.

Jimmy's embarrassment is total.

After awkwardly shuffling in his seat, he excuses himself, saying he needs the toilet.

Making his way down the carriage, he spies The Times newspaper open at the crossword on an empty seat; pauses to try and solve seven across: Former railway company leaving European Union.

An elderly gent in the opposite seat tells Jimmy he can have the paper, "I've read it"

"The crossword. You've not done it."

"No interest. Obviously, you have. Enjoy," the gent says, waving a hand at The Times.

"Oh," he adds, as Jimmy picks up the paper, "Good luck."

Jimmy thanks him, heads for the toilet. Re-emerges over ten minutes later causing Cissy to comment, when he sits down, "Where the heck have you been?"

"Trying to solve seven across," he replies, pointing at the crossword.

"Well, not trying. Not now. I HAVE solved seven across." He smiles with satisfaction.

Interupts Alfie who is reading a Michael Connelly novel: The Late Show. Asks the youngster if he does crosswords. Alfie answers in the affirmative. Jimmy clears his throat, spreads The Times on the table and shows him the crossword. Reads in a deliberate manner the seven across clue.

Alfie casually gives the answer, "Brexit."

A surprised Jimmy. "You don't hang about, lad. Took me ages to fathom it."

Cissy, without looking up from her book, "The old railway company is British Railways: BR. And exit is leaving. Brexit is leaving the EU."

Jimmy, exasperated, "I know that."

Silent pause before Jimmy tackles Alfie on the merits of leaving the EU.

Cissy swiftly brings the discussion to an end. "The

lad can do without your biased, departure views, Jimmy."

A smiling Alfie. "It's okay. I did the same as Jimmy."

"Voted to leave?" said Cissy.

"Yes."

Jimmy, a smirk across his face, turns to face his wife, who for once is not engrossed in her book. "Well, I never."

"I think we'll leave it there," says Cissy with finality.

Jimmy takes the hint, engages Alfie in conversation about crosswords and quizzes, the older man explaining how he loves Mastermind and University Challenge.

"And Pointless," adds Cissy.

Her husband scowls, refuses to react, expanding his views further."Of course, it's the general knowledge on Mastermind where I do better. Unless there's a specialist subject up my street."

"Like Nuclear Physics," says Cissy with heavy sarcasm.

Yet again Jimmy ignores her, continues, "What would your specialist subject be on Mastermind, lad?"

"Probably lawn tennis."

"Really?"

"Yes."

"Not music?"

"No."

"Oh."

After pausing for thought, Jimmy asks Alfie, "Which player won five consecutive Mens Singles Wimbledon titles?"

The youngster wonders where this is going, responds with, "Do you want to know? Or is it a question?"

Jimmy folds his arms, thinking he's got one over the lad. "I know the answer. Do you?"

Without hesitation, "Bjorn Borg."

Slightly miffed, the older man says, "Well, that was

an easy one. Just to get you started."

A succession of tennis related questions going back to the 1960s are all answered with relative ease by Alfie. Jimmy has to admit to himself that the young lad certainly knows his stuff. Cissy has been taking it all in, not even making any pretence of reading. She faces her husband, a wicked smile creasing her attractive features, unable to resist comment.

"Met your match there, Jimmy."

No time for Jimmy to respond as she faces Alfie. "Thinks he's a walking encyclopaedia."

Bit harsh, thinks Alfie, comes to Jimmy's defence.

"I'm sure he has other talents."

"Course I do," agrees Jimmy. "Or did. A tidy inside right when I was a young footballer. Midfielder to you, lad."

Having returned to her book, Cissy mutters more to herself than to Alfie. "His mother told me the only exercise he got was walking between the oche and the dartboard."

Alfie's had enough of this marital warfare and excuses himself, saying he needs a coffee before leaving the train.

Jimmy turns on his wife."Why do you have to keep chipping in with your two penneth all the time?"

Cissy places her book face down on the table. Jimmy has been wondering through the whole train journey what on earth has been keeping her absorbed.

Now all is revealed: MEN ARE FROM MARS, WOMEN ARE FROM VENUS by John Gray PhD.

A Practical Guide for Improving Communication and Getting What You Want In Your Relationship.

Cissy can see the intrigue in Jimmy's face. "So you've cottoned on have you?"

"Strange title. But what I'd like to say...

Cissy holds up a hand. "I think you've had quite a

big say during this journey. Now it's my turn."

Jimmy resigns himself to hearing her out. Rests his elbows on the table, clasps his hands together, using them as a prop for his chin. His wife points in the direction of Alfie's departure.

"That young lad, you've embarrassed him. Could see by his face. And you've embarrassed yourself even further, with your fanciful tales of injury spoiling your chances of playing professional football. Or laryngitis ruining your career as a pop singer. I know playing football for your scout troop doesn't sound as glamorous. But there it is. Or, it is what it is, as they say these days. Furthermore..."

Her flow is disturbed when she catches sight of a returning Alfie. Then, whispering to Jimmy, "The lad's back. Best behaviour."

As Alfie takes his seat, Cissy smiles, returns to her book. Jimmy stares out of the window. The youngster smiles at Cissy. But he senses something afoot. He plugs into his music, relaxes.

Later, this sea of tranquillity is punctured by an announcement as the train decelerates: "Your next stop is Stevenage. Stevenage is your next stop..."

The remainder of the announcement is lost in the noise of disembarking passengers gathering their belongings and making their way to the exits.

Alfie assembles all his possessions in readiness to leave the train. He shakes hands with Jimmy and Cissy, wishes them all the best and when the train comes to a standstill, follows the rest of the departing commuters.

Gazing out of the window, Jimmy says, with genuine feeling," A nice lad. He'll go far in life."

Cissy looks up from her book and joins her spouse in watching Alfie making his way towards the exit gates.

Suddenly, she jolts her head upwards towards the luggage rack, looks through the window, then up to the rack once more. She bumps Jimmy's arm as she stands.

"Ey up. Watch what you're doing, Cissy."

A quick riposte. "If you'd've been vigilant, you would've spotted this," said as she drags Alfie's cased violin from the luggage rack.

Jimmy stands. "Bloody hell. Give it here, Cissy."

"You'll never get..."

Jimmy doesn't allow his wife to finish. He is eager to do a good deed, redeem himself in Cissy's eyes. Snatches the case from her hands, rushes off the train.

Cissy watches events unfold through the window. Unfortunately, Alfie has disappeared from view. Jimmy pushes his way through the crowded platform, his eyes urgently seeking out the youngster.

A few moments of this before Cissy becomes aware of someone nearby: an anxious Alfie mutters, "Some sod's nicked my violin."

Cissy looks up at him. "No, lad. You forgot to take it from the luggage rack. Jimmy has it."

"Where is he?"

She points to a frustrated Jimmy, violin case in hand, still searching for its owner. Then a slow chugging sound as the train prepares to pull away from the platform. Alfie remains rooted to the spot, realises he's not going to be reunited any time soon with his beloved violin. Cissy half smiles as she views her bewildered husband, violin between his feet, his outstretched open hands, palms upward in a display of 'What the hell do I do now?' Gives a feeble wave to his wife as the train gathers momentum.

Cissy catches sight of her closed book, then a forlorn Jimmy and utters, "Just look at him. He wants to know everything and still knows nothing."

She pauses as Jimmy begins fading from view, adding, "The Martian has landed."

# KEEP ON RUNNING

I was desperate. No other word for it.
*Keep on running, keep on hiding*
*One fine day I'm gonna be the one*
*To make you understand...*

Easy money. That's what I was told. And that easy money would've got me out of a fix. A fix of my own making, admittedly.

Back to the beginning: My life was going nowhere. Nowhere. Not long after my demob from the army. I was one of the last National Service intake. Only saving grace: left the army with a healthy bank account. Most of my cash accrued during my posting in Germany.

My methods frowned upon by my superior officers: I was making rather a lot of money out of the German Army, who insisted the British Army take action against me. Which they did. But failed to get their hands on my capital. This surprised me. But impressed me at the same time.

Losing my sergeant's stripes was worth all the trouble. On demob I hooked up with a girl from East Yorkshire. Her father, Toby and his mate Mac planned to open their own betting shop within a workingman's club situated close to Hull Docks. And they were looking for further investment: enter yours truly.

A betting shop: making money from mugs. How could it go wrong?

Dropping hints to my girl, i.e, I wasn't short of a bob

or two. Worked a treat. I was in!

One of three partners: MacMillan, Palmer and Rice: Turf Accountants. That's me at the end: Les Rice.

Now I've always been partial to a punt myself: horses, cards, two flies crawling up a wall.

Being young, some would say daft, I didn't see the irony of one Les Rice, gambler, being a partner in a betting shop.

I only believed it when Toby and Mac employed a local signwriter to paint underneath the club's title, Riverview Social Club, the legend: incorporating MacMillan, Palmer and Rice, Turf Accountants. I was used to making money so I rather liked the word accountant. Had a nice ring to it.

Our enterprise was doing very well during the first six months or so. Very well indeed. In no small measure due to optimistic punters, usually dockers with Thursday pay packets tucked into their overall pockets, laying bets on rank outsiders i.e. horses with virtually no chance of winning a race. Of course, if one of these rank outsiders happened to win: happy days for the punter. Not so good for the bookie.

It was then I got to thinking. If I backed an outsider, with another bookie naturally, using a horse trainer mate of mine for inside info and I placed a decent amount of money on said outsider and it won, it would put MacMillan, Palmer and Rice in a very strong position.

Question was: where would I get the hefty wedge I needed to maximise the win? I'd used most of my savings for my investment in the business, so... Know what you're thinking. Same as me. Shouldn't have done. But it was with the best of intentions.

Okay, I'd have kept some of the winnings for the Les Rice Benevolent Fund. The bulk of my win would have benefited the business. Honest.

Anyway, I had no choice. So, when Toby and Mac

left one day after racing finished, I helped myself to a grand from our safe.

I knew I was safe - no pun intended - because Mac did our banking month end: twenty days to go. By month end though, the safe would contain forty grand.

Put the bet on Trip The Light Fantastic - could think of a better name for a horse - at a betting shop forty miles from ours, where nobody knew me.

Day of the race: final one at Haydock.

Fifteen runners. The favourite: Last Laugh. Aptly named as it happened: won by a short head. Leaving Trip The Light Fantastic in second place.

Yeah, I know. Should've backed it each way. But there you go.

As Toby once said to me, "You can't beat the bookie."

Nor can the bookie beat the bookie! Now I was really in the doodoo. Fortunately for me, or maybe unfortunately for me, I was born on a rough council estate in the north of England. Lived there for the first fifteen years of my life. And had mates who walked a very fine line between the legitimate world and the criminal world.

Day after Trip The light Fantastic let me down I drove to my old stamping ground and called on Russ Deighton. Three years older than me, already had a couple of spells in prison. But you'd want him on your side in a fight.

I was thinking maybe a loan. Prepared for high interest rate. But what choice did I have?

His proposition, his idea to get me out of the mess I created, knocked me off my feet: Russ said he'd pay me a grand, plus a £500 bonus, if I agreed to be the getaway driver on a town hall raid.

Russ and two mates planned to break into the town hall safe.

*Everyone is talking about me*
*It makes me feel so sad*
*Hey, hey, hey.*
*Everyone is laughing at me*

On the run for a week before I was arrested. Russ and his accomplices never made it to the getaway car.

"Lucky for you Russ Deighton and company are in a different prison to you, Les."

Looked at Seamus, one of the prison officers. A good lad was Seamus. He'll see me all right 'til 1968, when, hopefully, I'll be released. He understood my predicament.

"Aye, I'm due some good luck," I said.

A knock on my cell door.

Seamus in brief conversation with one of his colleagues, then turned to face me.

"You have visitors, Les."

Toby and Mac faced me across a table. An awkward silence seemed to last forever.

"Well say something," I said.

My partners, or should I say, ex partners, exchanged glances.

"I'll leave it to you, Mac. You're the company accountant," said Toby, a glower stretching across his swarthy features.

Mac had a more kindly, bespectacled face. Looked the younger man, though both were in their early fifties. Mac cleared his throat before speaking. This is bad news, I thought.

"We've been clearing your desk, Les. With you being... well, no longer a partner in the business. And..."

He fiddled about in his inside jacket pocket and pulled out a brown envelope.

Definitely bad news.

Mac handed me the envelope marked 'Les'.

"What's this?"

"Open it," ordered Toby.

Bloody hell!

Did as I was told.

Pulled out a betting slip from the envelope.

My handwriting: £12 win - Galloping Major – 3.15 York.

Mac simply said, "It won. Odds of a hundred to one."

Looked up from the slip at my former partners, my face breaking into a smile.

Then I laughed until tears rolled down my cheeks.

Edinburgh

# DAYDREAM BELIEVER

Another irritating call on his smart-phone. The same 02 London code.

That was what? Nine, ten calls in the past twenty-four hours. Three while he'd been enjoying, or trying to enjoy, a cool lager shandy to combat the warm August weather.

"Probably a scam, sir," commented the barman.

Ex Detective Chief Inspector Alec Rothwell briefly scowled at the youngster, who was prone to chipping in with unwanted observations.

Rothwell pocketed his phone, lifted his drink and chose a comfortable armchair well away from the well stocked bar.

He liked the Grand Hotel's 1906 Bar. Had done ever since promotion had presented itself and he'd come to live in York, working for the North Yorkshire Police, briefly interrupted with a short spell attached to the Met in London. His first twenty years of service were with the Lothian and Borders Police in his native Scotland. He saw the move south as a fresh challenge.

Unfortunately, along the way, the challenge included two more challenges: double matrimony. Both unsuccessful.

Part of the problem, no, most of the problems were caused by both of his ex's fondness for booze. Whereas Alec Rothwell was bordering teetotal.

While his younger colleagues were getting Brahms and Liszt, Rothwell moved steadily up the ranks, before finding contentment as a DCI.

Worked some high profile cases, particularly in the world of high finance. But not one for having his face splashed all over the tabloids, or on television.

His superiors could take the kudos. And all the associated grief from the crooks.

Neither of Rothwell's exes appreciated his point of view. Both wanted to bask in reflected glory.

The ex copper's service was drawing to a close when he began a relationship with South American beauty Bianca. His career was in cruise control and he'd promised a holiday anywhere she wished to go.

"Surprise me. You choose," she said to him.

He scrolled through holidays on his phone: French Riviera appealed. As did Scandinavia. Or New York.

California. Wanted to visit when he had a motorbike in his teens.

Route 66? No. Not relaxing.

After ten minutes or so his head was spinning. Too much choice.

He wished Bianca had surprised HIM.

Put down his phone, sipped his shandy and finally came to a decision: texted his girlfriend, asking her to be ready with a packed suitcase mid afternoon.

He'd pick her up and they'd drive to Manchester Airport, where together, they would choose a destination from the Departure Board.

On his way out of the Grand he crossed the barman's path.

"Any more scams, sir?"

Rothwell shook his head before heading for his midnight blue VW Golf. He turned left out of the car park, the beginning of his journey to Lancashire.

Gridlocked traffic in York, taking forty-five minutes to reach the city boundary and onto the A64.

Was it imagination? Paranoia? Or was it the instincts

of an experienced police officer?

Because Rothwell was almost certain he was being tailed: a red Audi behind within minutes leaving the Grand.

Not long and he was leaving the A64 for the A1 going south to Ferrybridge, where he intended to join the M62 to Manchester. Red Audi still behind, but trying to clock the registration number not proving easy because it was partly obscured by muck.

Ferrybridge Services gave Rothwell the opportunity to sus out the situation. Alighting from his car, his eyes searched the perimeters: no sign of the Audi.

"You definitely need a holiday, my son," the ex cop uttered to no one in particular.

"Pardon?"

Rothwell realised he'd voiced his thoughts out loud, bringing the query from a young man about to unlock his own car.

The older man smiled. "Just talking to myself, son. You get like that when you reach fifty years of age."

The youngster merely said, "Oh," made himself comfortable in his car and drove off.

Alec Rothwell was disappointed the lad hadn't said something on the lines of, "You don't look your age."

Viewing his appearance in the mirror of the Gents, his dark hair was showing slight signs of greying at the temples, but other than that he looked and felt in good shape. No use mentioning to the youngster that his second wife likened his looks to a young Sean Connery, because he'd probably think him a bighead. Not far from the truth, mind you.

He was casual smart today, but had a liking for sharp suits as well.

Rothwell munched his way through a chicken sandwich, washed down with a Coke. Felt more relaxed as he departed the restaurant, all the time, however, scanning his surroundings.

Not too far to his car, the glinting sun on the windscreen causing him to squint. Regretably, this gave an advantage to the female in the front passenger seat. He wondered why his car was unlocked. Now he knew.

The hard-faced middle-aged blonde, gun in hand, greeted him. "In case you are wondering, Mr Rothwell, I do know how to handle this gun," said with a heavy east European accent.

Cursed himself for letting his guard slip. With the Audi disappearing from view, he'd felt little danger.

"You in the red Audi?"

"Of course."

"What's this all about?"

"All I have to do is get you to Edinburgh. In one piece."

"Edinburgh?"

"Get your foot down and we can be there in two and half hours."

"I've got no show on at the Fringe."

"Drive."

He paused.

She pointed the gun at him.

Held up his hands in surrender, lowered them, turned the key in the ignition and pulled out of the car park.

A silent journey as he negotiated various turns to set them on the A1 north.

Rothwell eyed his kidnapper intently for a short while, aware he must keep focused on the road ahead.

"What?" the blonde said enigmatically.

Her driver was unsure if the utterance was one of interest in him, romantically.

"Look in the glove compartment. Pick out the Diana Krall CD 'Quiet Nights' – track seven."

She slotted the CD into the player.

Rothwell sang in unison with Krall:

*Este seu olhar quando*
*econtra o meu*
*Fala de umais coisas*
*Que eu no posso acreditar*
*Doce sonhar pensar que voce*
*Gosta de mim como eu de voce*

The woman turned down the volume. "I do not understand Spanish."

"Portuguese actually. I'll translate."

"What is this: Britain Got Talent?"

He ignored her and spoke the words of the song in English while holding eye contact with his adversary when safety permitted:

*Those eyes of yours*
*When they meet mine*
*Speak of things I cannot believe*
*Sweet is to dream and to think that you*
*Love me as much as I love you*

The former cop seemed to have embarrassed his companion. But she quickly regained her composure. "Try to catch me out, Scotsman?"

"Just aiming to make a long journey more pleasurable."

Prodded the gun into his ribs, "Drive."

Neither of them wanted a silent trip, so she agreed to the entire Diana Krall album being played. A wry smile from the blonde and indeed, Alec Rothwell when the singer seductively crooned:

*I've Grown Accustomed To His Face.*

Then: track five – Walk On By.

"That's what you should've done, wee lassie."

"Excuse me?"

"Listen to the words."

A pause.

"Very funny."

He thought it best to remain quiet for a while. His captor seemed content to listen to the music:

*We will live eternally in this mood of reverie*
*Away from all the earthly cares around us*

An interruption from Rothwell's phone nestling in the glove compartment, which Blondie opened.

Viewed the screen.

"Who is Bianca?" she enquired.

"My girlfriend. Can we stop. Need to explain"

"No explaining. Drive."

Not going well, he thought.

As the journey progressed Bianca made a further five attempts to contact her man.

This relationship was going to be better than his others.

She was THE ONE.

Bianca knows wife number two; of course she does, having introduced Alec to her.

As he and the alluring, bronzed beauty got to know each other better and as his police career drew to a close, he felt sure mistakes from the past would be buried. Once and for all. No more lengthy cases. No more long shifts. No more interrupted meals. No more early phone calls.

After their holiday in the sun, a fresh start in her native country appealed. That seemed a long way off as Rothwell and partner travelled through Northumberland, drizzle sliding down the windscreen.

Surprisingly though, she didn't object to further offerings from Diana Krall, or the tenor sax of Sonny Rollins. She did, however, object to a toilet stop.

"You think me stupid? Good time for you to make your escape."

Although the Scotsman was beginning to tire, Blondie wasn't, the gun still firmly in her grip. He was extremely relieved when the sign for Edinburgh came into view.

"Which part of Edinburgh?" he enquired.

"Portobello."

He glanced sideways, "Porty?"

"Porty?" she mimicked.

"That's what we know it as. Me. My family."

"You know it?"

"Know it? I was born there."

The blonde nodded. "I tell you when to stop."

Alec Rothwell steered his car through familiar territory, the A1 stretching into east Edinburgh, onto Portobello High Street, featuring the usual mix of charity shops, offices and takeaways.

Told to drop his speed to twenty miles an hour, he spotted the Foresters public house.

"Pull into a space past the bus stop," ordered the gun-woman.

As he pulled up the handbrake, a tap on his window.

His hazy point of view through the rain smeared window: a careworn, overcoat wearing bloke, mid-fifties, shaggy greying hair.

Made himself comfortable behind the driver's seat.

A clear view for Rothwell now: Vincent Sabbatini.

"How you doing, Detective Chief Inspector?" said in a vaguely recognisable Italian accent.

"EX DCI."

"Yeah. I heard. Thought you woulda made Super. Or Chief Super even."

"No desire to be in charge of pens and paper clips. Or wear a uniform."

"Anyway. You looka well. For retired man."

"Look after myself, Sabbatini. Gym, balanced diet, minimum alcohol intake. My ex, second ex, tells me I look like Sean Connery. A young Sean Connery."

"Shaun the Sheep more like it."

The blonde woman laughed as Rothwell responded, "Aye, well, down to business. You've not got me up here to stroll along Porty prom."

"I gave you good info. Many years, Alec. Saved your arse a couple of times."

"Aye, I'll give you that, probably best informant in the game."

"Probably? Definitely."

"What's this all about, Sabbatini?"

"Now is payback time."

Answer in a resigned voice, "Why didn't I think this day would ever come?"

"Day has arrived, Rothwell" interjected the blonde.

Half turning, the detective complaining to Sabbatini, "Who is this, Vincent?"

"My aide Malina."

"Aide? What the hell is your business now?"

"Don't laugh. I am now a PI."

"Private investigator. YOU?"

The Italian shrugged.

"It's official. You have an office?" enquired Rothwell.

"Back down the road, close to the Old Town Hall."

"How ironic."

"Ironic?"

"The Portobello Town Hall is now a police station."

Sabbatini shrugged as Rothwell added, "Church nearby as well. Couldn't make it up."

The PI put the former detective in the picture, literally, showing photos of a middle-aged, Scottish Nationalist MP, Sean MacLennan. Devout Catholic, son of a Northern Irishman, but born in Glasgow. Models himself on Ian Paisley. MacLennan's wayward, nineteen-year-old daughter, Flora, mixing with bad company.

"How bad?" asks Rothwell.

Sabbatini pulled no punches. "As bad as there is."

Sean MacLennan wants no adverse publicity and Alec Rothwell has to pull Flora apart from her undoubted criminal associates, in particular Billy Bowles, Edinburgh hardman and ten years older than his girlfriend.

Sabbatini transferred photographs of persons of interest to Rothwell's phone.

"Tell me, Vincent, is MacLennan a friend of yours?"

"Not a friend exactly. More of a drinking companion."

"Thought he was God fearing"

"Vicars and priests drink. Anyway, he's more of a social drinker. Never seen reeling out of the Foresters."

"Your local?"

"We meet there occasionally."

"And he asked you to investigate his concerns?"

"Kind of."

"Why didn't you investigate, Sabbatini. As a concerned citizen?"

The Italian was non-committal.

"Already, Vincent, I am not liking what you asking me to do."

Blondie prods Rothwell with her gun as Sabbatini said, "I'm not asking you, I'm..." He and Rothwell, in unison, finish off the sentence, "...telling you."

"As I said earlier, Alec: you owe me."

The ex copper held his hands up in surrender.

"Okay. But I need a good night's sleep before I start. And before you mention it, I'm not kipping down in your office."

"No problem. Wherever you stay, keep a low profile. For three days. No shaving, no hair washing, none of your fancy clothes. You need to blend into Flora

MacLennan's scene. And stay away from her father. Come see me in my office after three days."

Sabbatini moved out of the car.

His aide followed suit.

Alec Rothwell watched them enter the Foresters public house prior to driving the short distance to Brunstane Road.

After parking his car he climbed several steps to the front entrance of the B & B and rang the door bell.

A swift response.

Still the same youngish Glaswegian who accommodated him in 2015, now sporting a full gingery beard.

Despite Edinburgh Fringe patrons utilising every available bed in the city Dougie had a room available.

Ex -Detective Chief Inspector Alec Rothwell fell onto his bed fully clothed and was asleep within a minute.

Eleven am the following day: a knock on Rothwell's door. Yawning, rubbing his eyes, he answered: Dougie with a coffee and brown buttered toast.

"Did nae wake you earlier. You seemed shattered last night."

Rothwell thanked him and asked if Dougie minded if he stayed in his room for the day.

"Nae problem. Plenty of books in the lounge next door. And CDs if you fancy music."

With that Dougie departed, leaving his guest to his own devices.

First was a visit to the bathroom: filled the wash-hand basin with hot water ready for a shave.

No razor.

Then he remembered: no shaving, no hair washing.

Viewed himself in the mirror: suitably scruffy already.

Wouldn't come easy to Rothwell, someone who had

always prided himself on being immaculately dressed.

His thoughts were interrupted by his ringing smart phone resting on the bedside unit.

Picked it up, answered, “Oh God. I’m so sorry Bianca.”

He let her rant on in Portugese for a while.

“A calme-se, Bianca,” he said softly when she paused for breath.

“Okay, I calm down,” quickly followed by “Porque voce ignora minhas ligacoes,” in a high-pitched voice.

Rothwell stayed calm.

“I’ve already told you: I was forced, at gunpoint, to drive up here. To Scotland.”

Bianca then became hysterical.

He let her rant and rave, holding his phone away from his ear, then responded when she’d run out of breath.

“I’m okay. Have to do a favour for an old friend. Should be home within a week, maybe less. Then we holiday.”

“Promessa?”

“Promise. I’ll keep in touch.”

He ended the call before Bianca went on another rant.

* * *

He’d quite enjoyed the three-day interlude, catching up on reading a couple of Ian Rankin novels, listening to Diana Krall on his phone, the occasional stroll on Portobello’s promenade.

Sent Sabbatini a text to let him know he’d be with him mid afternoon after buying his ‘new’ wardrobe at a nearby charity shop.

Sabbatini looked the ex-detective up and down: fashionably, torn denims, creased dark blue linen shirt and short casual, well-worn suede jacket.

“Scruffy enough?” said Rothwell.

The Italian shrugged, paused for thought, and then uttered, "Strange seeing you like that, Alec. Not used to it."

"You said..."

Sabbatini held up a hand. "You'll do fine. Look like a Drugs Squad detective."

Pause.

"You never made it to Drugs did you?" the Italian added.

Rothwell sat on the edge of a large mahogany desk littered with files, papers and a laptop.

"Are you kidding, Vincent? Those guys are lunatics. Battering down doors, kicking the crap out of innocent people, coshing anyone in their way with batons."

"The Flying Squad eluded you as well."

"The Sweeney were just as crazy as the Drugs mob. I preferred the collar and tie investigations."

"Nicking accountants, eh?"

"You were no accountant, Sabbatini."

"Robbery without violence. But I gave you good info."

"So you keep telling me. Just as I keep reminding you I kept you out of jail."

Sabbatini used his elbows to lean on his desk. "We're digressing, Rothwell. I have not invited you here for trip into memory lane."

As the private investigator detailed what was required of the ex copper, Alec Rothwell surveyed the office: obviously had once been some sort of shop, with shelving fixed to the wall opposite the desk,.behind which was an open entry leading to a small kitchen, two filing cabinets to Sabbatini's left, all walls painted in a pale dingy green colour and grey vinyl flooring under his feet.

It was oft used phrase, but 'down at heel' was the only one to describe Sabbatini's place of work.

"Know what you are thinking," said the Italian, adding, "This office is functional."

Leant further forward onto his desk. "You know Royal Mile Tavern?"

"Course I do."

"Billy Bowles regular drinker. Most nights. If you need to talk with him – before ten."

"What happens after ten?"

"Live music."

Rothwell nodded. "Does Bowles have form?"

"Nothing big: petty theft, causing disturbance, being drunk and disorderly."

"Minor stuff then. So minor has to become major."

"You got it."

"And Flora MacLennan. The Tavern her local too?"

"Mainly weekends."

* * *

Rothwell walked the short distance to the Golden Bite, ordered fish and chips to take out and took it onto Portobello's prom, sitting on a bench seat to consume them.

He gulped down a cooled down take-out tea from a cardboard cup after his meal, placed the cup alongside his thigh. Deep in thought, he was surprised by a youngster depositing a handful of coins into the cup.

As the youngster walked away he turned, "You could've said thank you."

The former cop looked up, then viewed the money inside the cup, realising the contributor was under the mistaken impression that Rothwell was a beggar. "Thank you son," he called out.

This resulted in a thumbs up from the lad.

"God, I must look bad," Rothwell exclaimed to himself.

Or good, in Sabbatini's view.

Stretched his arms across the back of the bench and watched the gentle waves lapping the beach.Took out his smartphone and punched in Sabbatini's number. Didn't have to wait long for an answer, "Now what?"

"You said I could resolve the situation any way I like. Does that mean I can resolve it quickly. In one night?"

"Whatever. You're in charge, Rothwell."

"I may have to take a beating. But the sooner I'm in sunnier climes, the better."

"Whatever."

"So, to sum up Sabbatini: the rules are – there are no rules."

"Be careful." And with that the PI ended the call.

Rothwell checked his watch: too early to call in at the Royal Mile Tavern.

Contemplated a swim. Cold in the sea, but could use the nearby indoor pool. Instead he settled for a barefoot walk along the beach, now and again treading water: definitely too cold for a swim.

A streak of sunlight filtered through the clouds as he watched the world go by from his seat on the wall separating the prom from the beach; he offered his face up to the warmth, imagining himself sunbathing alongside Bianca on the white sand of a South American resort.

The noise of a skateboarder jolted the ex detective from his reverie.

Nearly six in the evening. Been a while since he'd visited the Foresters public house, or, to give the place its fancy new title: Guild of Foresters. But to Rothwell it would always be the Foresters Arms.

He pushed his way through the timber-glass panelled entrance and was faced with the new decor: timber flooring, exposed brick walls, small tables teamed with purple and blue bucket seats which gave the pub a modern feel.

A fair few people tucked into food, tempting a hungry Rothwell to sample a chicken dish.

He eagerly ate his meal while slowly sipping a Coke, keeping his eyes on the entrance. And minutes after he mopped up the last of his food, a tallish, middle-aged gent with grey hair clipped short, entered. He was smartly dressed in a navy suit.

The barman could be heard saying,"Good evening, Mr MacLennan. What can I get you ?"

Rothwell wandered over to the bar, MacLennan moving to allow the ex cop to order, bringing an appreciative response, "Thank you. Gentlemen are far and few between these days. Can I get you a drink?"

MacLennan smiled. "Thanks, but I have a drink coming."

Ordering a Coke on ice, Rothwell stayed put, engaged the politician in general chit-chat.

Several minutes later, when turning to view the clientle, an annoyed looking Sabbatini motioned with his head for his employee to follow him outside.

"Are you innocent? Or just stupid?" uttered the Italian.

"Stupid."

Sabbatini pointed to the pub. "You don't go in there quizzing MacLennan. In fact you do nota go in there full stop."

"All right, all right."

A voluptuous youngish blonde alighted from a taxi and linked arms with Sabbatini.

She looked admiringly at Rothwell before speaking in an Italian accent, "And who is a your friend, Vincent?"

"Alec. He's Scottish."

Smiling seductively at Rothwell, "I like Scotland."

Admiring her low cut dress, he uttered, "And

Scotland likes you."

Sabbatini yanked his girlfriend's arm, "Dai Claudia. Non piaci solo alla Scozia."

Rothwell's response was cut short by Claudia as she entered the pub with her beau. "Vincent is jealous."

Alec Rothwell crossed to the other side of the road and waited at the bus stop.

Wasn't too long before a crimson Lothian bus, number 26 stopped for him to get on. Being Friday night it was a slow journey into Edinburgh city centre. And the Festival was in full flow.

Rothwell elected to leave the bus early and undertake a gentle stroll to the Royal Mile Tavern.

The gentle stroll, however, turned out to be anything but, as he had to push his way through milling crowds, many of whom were spending time in the Scottish capital to enjoy the festivities.

Street entertainers were a plenty and though he'd taken pleasure in past Festival Fringes, the ex copper's focus was on completing the task set by Vincent Sabbatini.

St.David's Street. Then North Bridge. The Carlton Hotel edged into view. A left hand turn onto the Royal Mile.

A Sixties song, Daydream Believer, played by a brass band filled the air, some of the crowds singing along. But then it was Friday night.

As Rothwell set foot inside the Royal Mile Tavern he almost bumped into Billy Bowles, who was moving away from the bar holding a pint of lager and what looked like a G and T.

A hard man. That was what Sabbatini had told him.

He looked it: met Rothwell's height, close shaved head,pointed features, with obligatory 'hard man' neck and arm tattoos, face set in a permanent sneer.

It appeared the Tavern drinkers accorded Bowles

some kind of respect, allowing him to make his way through the throng unhindered.

Flora MacLennan took hold of her drink, with what seemed to Rothwell, a nervous smile playing across her pretty face, framed by tousled, shoulder length light brown hair.

Her clothing was striking by its simplicity: short-sleeved white linen top paired with tight fitting black jeans tucked into ankle boots.

Rothwell felt a sharp dig between his shoulder blades, followed by thick west Scots coast accent, "Ye wanting a drink? Or are you just admiring the view?"

The ex-cop turned, facing a pock marked, ruddy, middle-aged man, who was possibly an associate of Bowles. An apology was offered and accepted. It wasn't this man Rothwell wanted an argument with.

On his turn at the bar, Rothwell asked for an iced Coke, found himself a suitable space to keep Flora in his eyeline.

The mass of bodies inside the pub forced him a little nearer to where Flora sat, seemingly in a world of her own.

Twenty minutes or so passed by. With her elbows on the table, Flora began applying lipstick. Bowles was too busy to notice when she lost her grip on the cosmetic, which fell onto the timber flooring. The ex cop seized his opportunity to ingratiate himself with the young lassie, picking up the lipstick, smiling kindly as he handed it back to her.

She returned his smile and thanked him, uttering, possibly for the benefit of the company she was keeping, "Thank you so much. Nice to meet someone with manners for a change."

"You're welcome, bonny lass," said Rothwell, loud enough to attract the attention of nearby Billy Bowles.

Flora smiled once more, warmly.

Didn't go unnoticed by her boyfriend, who immediately rose to his feet, knocking over his chair in the process, facing Rothwell, their noses almost touching. "Did ye not see the sign on the door as ye came in," said Bowles, in a sarcastic tone, with menacing overtones.

Rothwell gulped, feeling genuinely threatened.

"Sign?"

Bowles looked over his shoulder at his coterie of mates grinning. "Aye. No scruffbags, druggies, winos, or down and outs allowed in here."

Now was Rothwell's chance. Now or never. Would be painful. But. Hopefully. Job done.

* * *

Couldn't get the song out of his head:

*You once thought of me*
*As a white knight on his steed*
*Now you know how happy I can be*

*Oh what can it mean to be a*
*Daydream believer...*

Rothwell's eyes flickered: a hazy overcoated figure hovered at the end of his bed.

Bed?

Eyes now fully focused: Sabbatini.

"Good to see you out of Intensive Care, Alec."

Alec Rothwell recalled nothing of Intensive Care. But knew now he was lying in a hospital bed.

"You don't remember?" enquired the Italian.

"How long have I been here?"

"Four days ICU, one day where you are now. Should be home in two weeks"

"I remember a brass... no, silver band playing. A Monkees song...?"

"Ah yes. You keepa singing this... Believer."

"Daydream Believer."

Rothwell paused for thought.

"Remember Bowles. Yes... I remember."

"My man said you took a beating. Your plan. Yes?"

"Bit fuzzy."

"You said a to me: you may have to take a beating."

"I did?"

"You did. And it worked. Flora MacLennan has split from Billy Bowles after what he did to you. Don't look in a mirror for a while."

Rothwell half smiled through a bruised and battered face. Then, picking up on what Sabbatini said moments earlier, "Your man. What man?"

"Had you tailed. He saw everything at the Tavern. And outside. And before you ask, he stepped in to stop Bowles killing you."

"That's why I was in Intensive Care and not the morgue."

"Exactly."

"Don't know whether to thank you. Or thank your man."

"No problemo."

"That was a joke," said Rothwell with a grimace.

"You said the rules are - there are no rules," remarked Sabbatini.

Rothwell held up a hand in acknowledgement. After a pause he added, "I take it Sean MacLennan is satisfied?"

"Totalmente."

"That's something. And Flora has definitely broken up with Bowles?"

"Already told you, Alec. Yes. And the court will make sure they are apart for quite some time."

"How satisfied is Sean MacLennan?"

"Ah. You are talking about your fee."

"I'd hate to think I was battered for nothing."

Rothwell's phone, which was resting on his bedside table rang, struggled to pick it up.

Sabbatini obliged and handed it over. The ex detective checked the screen, pulled a face.

"What is wrong, Alec?"

"It's Bianca."

Within a minute the call ended, but was then replaced with Facetime: Bianca once more.

A deliriously happy South American beauty, "Alec. Boas nova."

"Good news?"

"Eu reservei um feriado. Para o Havai. Vamos dois dias."

"Whoa. Slow down, Bianca. Tell me in English."

"Okay. I book. For me, for you........ holiday. Hawaii. Two days we go. For two weeks."

Rothwell surveys his habitat: a hospital side ward. With the distraction of Sabbatini's entrance, he'd not noticed the saline drip he was hooked up to. Or the nearby pile of medication. His head began throbbing, phone dropped onto the bedspread.

"Alec?"

He retrieved his phone.

"About Hawaii, Bianca. Thing is..."

# SOMETHING IN THE AIR

*Call out the instigators*
*Because there's something in the air*
*We've got to get together sooner or later...*
*The revolution's here*
*And you know that it's right*

The song had been a favourite in the pub last night. Catchy – undoubtedly. Its meaning: God knows.

Whatever. Couldn't get it out of my head. A head full of fuzziness. Not a heavy drinking session, but enough to break my golden rule: minimum alcohol intake night before a match. And on this particular Sunday morning I felt sluggish, older than my twenty-three years.

The folks were away for the weekend, so relied on the alarm to wake me up. Hated morning kick-offs. Could only face a tea and slice of buttered toast after I dressed. Then I put my boots, blue socks and white shorts into my holdall.

Checked my watch: 9.15. A few minutes later I heard the sound of my mate Terry's motorbike. Locked the front door, took the spare helmet off him, jumped on the back of his Triumph 750 and we were away.

Away. Indeed we were. Playing away at Brunswick, thirteen miles east of the city. Brunswick had walloped our team, Carlton Athletic 6-1 on our own pitch, last match of last season. Now, six weeks into the 1969/70 season, was an early chance of revenge.

When I tell strangers I play for Carlton Athletic, they

assume I play for the professional league club Charlton Athletic.

Easy mistake. And I do nothing to rectify this assumption. Me and Terry work for Carlton Engineering, hence our team's name.

Might be early October, but there's a nip in the air. Terry takes it steady, possibly because of last night's session. But also because it's not all that long ago the breathalyser was introduced. Good to breathe in the country air as we leave the city behind.

When we arrive at Brunswick's ground most of the lads are there. And, thankfully, so is Ced, our ageing manager, also responsible for laundering our mid blue shirts.

Being an Everton fan, I love our kit. It was touch and go last season whether we were prepared to keep Ced on as manager, or give him the boot (pardon the pun) after he'd forgotten to bring our shirts for one of our away games.

Luckily for the team, or unluckily, the opposition had a spare set of shirts: stretched down to our knees, lace-up collars and, according to the opposing team captain, originated from the 1930s.

We looked a right bunch of nanas in very wide blue and white stripes instead of our own kit.

Brunswick's ground was typical of country villages: not much better than a ploughed field. Maybe that's an exaggeration. But, usually the grass needs a good cut. Also, we always expect their team to remove several cow pats from the pitch. The changing room wasn't up to much either: a glorified shed, no showers.

Within ten minutes of Terry parking his bike, all of our team, plus substitute, and two standbys had arrived.

No opposition yet. But not unusual for Brunswick to arrive with little time to spare.

Then we spied an old codger, tugging his flat cap

tighter on top of his head, walking his black and white collie. Came into view far side of the field via a gap in a hedgerow. Could see he was approaching us, a smile creasing his features.

"You lads are a bit early," he said in a flat Lancashire accent.

"Early?" I uttered.

"Aye. Early. Brunswick always kick off at two o'clock this time o' year."

"You're kidding," cut in Terry.

"I'm not kidding, lad."

"Bloody marvellous," exclaimed one of the Sykes brothers.

"This is your bloody doing Ced," added the younger Sykes brother. "A bloody fiasco with those shirts. Now this"

I advocated calm, motioning with downward movements of my hands. "There's nothing we can do to change the kick-off time. Just have to accept it"

"Bloody marvellous," parroted Cliff, the older Sykes brother.

"What do you suggest we do?" said Nobby Sykes.

"I've got an idea," Barney Roberts, our goalkeeper, cheerfully said.

Barney, a big lad, strode over to the dog walker and asked him what time The Travellers' Rest, the nearby pub opened.

The old man pondered the question, brought his dog to heel and answered Barney's query.

"Ted, the landlord, opens up at twelve o'clock Sundays. But I'm sure he'll not turn down extra trade. On the quiet like. You'd not have to attract the attention of the local bobby though."

"Sounds good to me," responded Barney.

The old man beamed: must be on a back-hander from the landlord. "Let me have a word with Ted."

And off he toddled.

"Everyone's a winner," added Barney.

I wasn't so sure that would turn out to be the case.

Our goalie had a fondness for hand-pulled Tetleys bitter.

Terry's grimace let me know he agreed with me.

Most of the other lads were jubilant, particularly the Sykes brothers, who made their way briskly towards The Travellers' Rest, from where the old man appeared, giving a thumbs up.

As our team entered the pub we were greeted by Ted, a chunky, fair-headed chap in his mid-forties, ruddy complexion, indicating his own fondness for the booze.

Barney shook his hand vigorously, earning our goalie the first drink.

Next in line were the Sykes brothers, Cliff proclaiming, "Think of this session as team bonding."

Terry nudged me, whispering, "He's been reading one of those arty-farty psychology books."

Me and Terry were last to be served, both electing Cokes, which brought derision from the Sykes.

When boisterousness began creeping into the proceedings, Ted urged us to be quiet, saying his licence was at risk if PC Arnold Braithwaite sussed any out of hours drinking.

As the clock behind the bar nudged closer to 1.20 I could see more than half the team were worse for wear. Strangely enough, I wasn't feeling too clever myself and took myself off to the Gents for a cold water wash.

When I returned to the bar, Terry slanted his head towards me, indicating I should join him. He held up my third glass of Coke, asking me to sniff it. Which I did.

Now I knew why I felt rather giddy.

"Some bugger's spiked our drinks," Terry informed me.

Looked towards the Sykes brothers, a couple of Jack the Lads, whom I never warmed to. And never socialised with. I got along with them on the pitch. But that was it.

Cliff Sykes never forgave me for an incident during one of our Thursday training sessions last season: Ced announced the team for the following Sunday. Nobby Sykes wasn't in it.

Bringing about a childish outburst from his brother: "I'm not playing if our kid isn't playing."

I have to say, Nobby Sykes was nowhere near as good as Cliff. Though it pains me to say it. Although pushing thirty years of age he was, is, a very good player. And Nobby had had a run of very poor games.

Anyway, I looked at Cliff and said, "You're not playing if your kid isn't playing. How old are you?

With that, Cliff lunged towards me before being dragged away by Terry, who's not as big as Barney by any stretch of the imagination.

Barney is a man mountain. But still, Terry is quite tall and hefty, in a muscley sort of way.

I had to hand it to Ced: he stood his ground.

Nobby didn't play the following Sunday. Did him good though, making him work harder in training, before breaking back into the team six weeks later, due to his replacement being injured.

Terry restrained me from tackling the Sykes.

"Do your tackling on the pitch," he told me.

Famous last words.

Brunswick were going through their warm up on the pitch when we left, some staggered out of the pub. Barney was particularly worse for wear as we trudged over to the changing room. Within ten minutes we were ready for action.

Ced gathered us all together, a dismayed look creasing his features below his perennial flat cap.

He'd not been party to the drinking session. Pity Barney had not followed suit.

"Okay, lads," Ced uttered.

He paused. For thought? Inspiration?

"Okay, lads," he repeated, "Pretend you're Juventus."

"Fray Bentos more like it," I chipped in.

Even the Sykes brothers laughed.

"Okay, lads" from Ced for a third time. "All we can do is play a containing game."

"Meaning?" enquired Terry.

Ced looked incredulous. "Meaning defend with your lives and hope we get a nil-nil draw out of the game."

The team knew that, with Terry's six foot two stature and bulky frame, most of the defending would be down to him.

Both teams lined up, me in my usual number ten position.

The referee surveyed the motley group of players known as Carlton Athletic, probably lost for words. He was. And remained silent.

Blew his whistle for the start of the match.

Brunswick, urged on by around forty or fifty fans, most of them I would say from the farming community, green wellies in evidence. And, as befits the North, cloth caps in abundance, even on the women.

The match was an uphill battle from the start, the uneven pitch churning up due to heavy rain the past few days. Terry his usual dependable self, winning most of the airborne balls. The revelation though was Barney, our inebriated goalkeeper, some of his saves bordering on the miraculous.

On one occasion, when I retrieved the ball for a throw-in, a nearby Ced commented, to no one in particular, "Should 'ave a skinful before every game."

I smiled: indeed he should. Based on current

evidence.

Carlton Athletic, unbelievingly, and much to the annoyance of their Barbour coated supporters, managed to keep the game scoreless until the closing minutes. Don't think we'd had a shot on target, due to defending en masse. Although I did shave the upright from distance. I was huffing and puffing, mainly because my teammates saw me as the lone attacker. This involved chasing long balls hoofed forty yards or more up the pitch. For God's sake, referee, blow the final whistle.

My last memory of the match was Cliff Sykes taking a corner kick from the right hand side. Followed by pandemonium in and around the penalty area, the ball ping-ponging all over the place.

Think it was during this chaos that I passed out. Apparently, Terry had piggy-backed me into the pub landlord's living room. My mate looked down at me spreadeagled, still in footy gear, on a large settee, a big, beaming smile crumpling his face.

"What are you so happy about?" I enquired.

He stooped lower, grabbed hold of my shoulders,. "We did it" Terry exclaimed. "You did it"

I was puzzled. "What you going on about?"

"A fluke admittedly. But they all count."

"What?"

"Before you flaked out. The ball hit your knee and went past their goalie."

The Humber

# FOR ONCE IN MY LIFE

January 1979

A bitterly cold day.

A raw north-easterly sweeping off the River Humber. Made bearable by the dazzling sunshine. What was not bearable was the pitifully low number of mourners attending the funeral of my life-long friend and business partner, Toby. Even his younger brother was absent.

If I thought the turnout was low in chapel, it was lower still at a nearby pub for the wake. Ironically, I was reminded of a favourite adage of Toby's, "Everyone loves you when you're dead. The chapel will be packed to the rafters."

After spending some time with my old mate's family, made my way to the exit as the song on the juke-box resounded from the bar area.

Voice to my left, local accent, "Hello, Mac, 'ow you doing?"

"Arthur," I said, "long time, no see."

We shook hands, wished each other a belated "Happy New Year."

He'd not changed much. Even though he was pushing forty years of age. Remained a tall, slim, fair haired, clean-cut bloke. Smart as always, wearing a dark grey suit, teamed with immaculate white shirt, black tie.

Then we faded back ten years. Back to the fag end of the so-called Swinging Sixties.

January 1969:

A quiet afternoon in MacMillan and Palmer, Turf

Accountants, the business being located inside The Riverview Social Club. Goes without saying dockers made up much of our clientele.

Foul weather had curtailed the horse racing, leaving only a sprinkling of punters optimistically studying the form in various publications.

In the absence of placed bets, I caught up with some paperwork.

My partner, Toby, fiddled about by himself on the snooker table.

Observed his profile, illuminated by the strip light hanging over the table, over which he stretched to pot two red balls simultaneously; uncannily resembled the film actor Clark Gable.

A recent customer of ours, Arthur, sat at a corner table, worry and anxiety etched across his face, his mood not made better by the music he'd selected on the juke-box, A Stevie Wonder number:

*For once in my life I won't let sorrow hurt me,*
*Not like it hurt me before...*

Studied the two men briefly: Toby, a contented, reasonably successful businessman in late middle-age. And Arthur, a young chap struggling to look after his wife and two kids, his occupational income from sales heavily dependent on commission.

Toby went over to the youngster, consoled him, knowing Arthur would regale him with the same old story: his wife couldn't cope with the meagre income he brought home each week, putting a strain on their marriage, causing bitter arguments and consequently leading to demands from creditors, some of whom distressed his wife by using 'doorstepping' methods.

Of course, reckless gambling didn't help. We tried to advise him. To our cost sometimes,but to no avail.

The previous week had been his wife, Betty's birthday. To show his devotion, Arthur bought her a Stevie Wonder long playing record. 'For Once In My Life' was the track dedicated to her. Obviously, it had not had the desired effect.

After a brief chat with Arthur, my partner and mate wandered over to our 'office' situated behind the grilled counter. Ran a hand through his dark hair, stubbed out his cigarette in a nearby ashtray. "What we're gonna do about Arthur I don't know, Mac."

I closed the ledger I'd been working on, lit up myself. "Short of him winning the pools, there's nothing we can do."

Checked my watch. "Anyway, what's he still doing here? His wife will..."

Toby quickly cut in. "Late tea tonight. Betty's taking the kids swimming."

Looked over Toby's shoulder. He turned to see what I was looking at: Arthur approaching. A half smile across his glum face as he addressed Toby.

"Fancy a game of snooker? Just to while away the time until Betty gets home with the sprogs."

Always willing to oblige, Toby accompanied Arthur as they walked over to the snooker table. A good-natured game ensued. A handful of people inside the club took little notice, most of them still concentrating on their newspapers, the Racing Post prominent, although darkness and adverse weather had ended all race meetings for the day.

I returned to my admin work, calculating winning bets. Didn't take too long, so I sat myself close to the snooker table, on which Arthur set up the balls for another game.

Looking intently at his opponent, "Shall we make it interesting, Toby?"

Toby glanced my way, then stared resolutely at

Arthur.

"What?" said the young man.

Toby lit up.

It was up to me to let Arthur know the score.

"If by interesting, Arthur, you mean playing for money. Forget it. Toby is..."

"Mac, I'm a grown up. I can make my own decisions."

"I know. But..."

Threw my hands up in despair. The lad was either a non-runner or a dark horse.

Toby glanced my way once more, blowing smoke through his nose. Seemed I needed to press home the point. "Toby has a sideboard full of trophies at home and...

Arthur didn't want advice.

"Let me ask Toby straight. Are you chicken?"

Toby stubbed out his cigarette on the linoleum floor before emptying the snooker table pockets and arranging the balls on the green baize for the start of an 'interesting' game. I shrugged with resignation. Toby saw me, raised his eyebrows in surrender.

"Shall we say ten pounds to the winner?" Arthur exclaimed hopefully.

Toby did not argue.

Despite a valiant effort, Arthur narrowly lost the game. Only because, in my opinion, my old mate took it easy.

As Arthur set up the table for another game, "Got to admit, I was unlucky," more to himself than us.

"Ten again?" directly to Toby, who merely nodded in agreement.

The second encounter showed Arthur's luck didn't come into it He was beaten with ease, sending a message to the younger man that he was chucking away money he could ill afford to.

Sprang from my seat. Arthur held up a hand, refusing further advice. Felt for the lad. But more than that, felt for his wife. Toby began moving away from the scene of his victories. Arthur barred his way.

Was almost nose to nose with his adversary. "You've got to give me a chance to..."

"Lose more money?"

Resisted the temptation to come between them, but calmly said to Arthur, "Leave it alone, son."

He ignored me, addressed Toby, "Double or quits?"

Toby had been placed in an impossible situation. With reversed roles he'd want that option. But...

Following a brief pause, considering his dilemma, Toby slowly triangled the red balls on the table, then positioned the colours appropriately on their spots. He took hold of his cue in readiness for the opening shot.

Toby split the reds, purposely in my view, to leave Arthur a reasonable chance of potting a red. This he did. Followed up with a break of forty.

Toby matched his break. It was then nip and tuck for a quarter of an hour, both men producing snookers. Then Arthur went on a run with a break approaching fifty. Suddenly, he stopped, holding his cue, rifle style, by his side.

He eyeballed Toby steadfastly. "I know what you're doing. And I don't like it."

"Excuse me?"

"Don't want you holding back. Making it easy for me."

He'd sussed his rival out

Laconic as ever, Toby stood aside and let Arthur continue. Because of his protest, he'd lost some rhythm in his game, only adding four to his break before hitting a poor shot.

Toby shot a downcast, cursory glance my way. I knew exactly how this 'double or quits' game would pan out. And so it proved. Toby annihilated his young opponent in double quick time.

A crestfallen Arthur pulled his wallet out of the inside pocket of his jacket, handed his senior four crisp ten pound notes. At a guess, probably near enough his pay packet for the week.

My partner stuffed the money in his back trouser pocket, gave Arthur a comforting pat on the shoulder.

A blast of cold air penetrated the premises. We all looked to the double-door entrance: Bunny Butler, attired in his customary navy blue, pinstriped, three piece suit, dark blue shirt and tie came over to greet us. He had the appearance of a gangster. And rumour had it, prior to moving north from London's East End, he was acquainted with the Kray twins, the notorious Sixties hoodlums.

The owner of Riverview, which housed our betting shop, was all handshakes and back slaps.

"All right, Arthur? You look a bit down in the dumps."

To save Arthur's embarrassment, I intervened. "He's had a setback. We'll leave it there."

"Buy the lad a drink, Butts. Cheer him up a bit," added Toby.

Bunny preferred Butts. For obvious reasons.

"No problem. We'll all have one. Toast the New Year."

Scotches all round. With Butts making sure our depressed companion's was laced with water. Last thing Arthur needed was the breathalyser on his way home.

My turn to drive so nursed a tot. Toby regaled us with a couple of light-hearted stories; never knew for sure if they were true or not. Still, on a cheerless January evening, everyone needs light in their lives.

After a while Butts excused himself, telling us he had some business to attend to in his office.

Arthur retreated to his preferred corner table and consoled himself with another whisky, giving me no choice but to insist I give him a lift home.

Me and Toby cashed up and stashed the day's takings in the safe. We then pulled on our overcoats, buttoned them up and knotted our scarves. Regarded Arthur deep in thought, running a finger around the edge of his glass.

"Ready son?" I said.

"If you don't mind I'll stay awhile. Get Butts to drive me home."

Wagging a finger at him, "Make sure you do."

He looked up, smiled weakly. Toby and I exchanged concerned glances before bidding him goodnight.

My mate halted at the exit. "Hang on a minute, Mac."

Purposefully, he strode over to where Arthur was sitting. For some reason the lad stood up, as if expecting something untoward.

Don't know what I was expecting – a lecture on the perils of gambling from someone who knows what they are, to someone who doesn't?

Whatever, I wasn't expecting what I actually witnessed: from his back trouser pocket, Toby removed the four ten pound notes Arthur had given him earlier and shoved them into the breast pocket of the lad's jacket.

"Next time you play snooker for money, son, make sure you can actually play the game."

January 1979

Arthur suggested a catch up about old times. In the bar. Preferred bars to lounges, he said, adding I would have to visit him in York, where he now lived and worked. "Roaring coal fires, stone floors and beams. Can't beat it."

With that he popped over to the juke-box and selected a song while I got the drinks in.

Called over to me, "Listen to the words, Mac."

*I don't care what you say anymore this is my life*
*Go ahead with your own life, leave me alone*
*I never said you had to offer me a second chance*
*I never said I was a victim of circumstance*

As Billy Joel continued singing, Arthur joined me at the bar. Reminded me of his contest with Toby on the snooker table all those years ago. And his generous gesture.

"Changed my life, Mac. Changed my life."

After reminiscing for twenty minutes or so, I told Arthur I would have to be on my way; needed to prepare for the business of the day at my betting shop.

Arthur finished his drink, "Aye. Same here."

As we made our way out of the pub, "Same here?"

"Aye. I own three betting shops in York."

Arthur smiled modestly, warmly shook my hand before speeding off in his BMW Series 3 saloon.

Who said gambling doesn't pay!

# A HARD DAY'S NIGHT

It had been a quiet week. End of February and virtually a full, twenty-eight days of bitterly cold weather. In my job you have to be prepared and put up with whatever comes your way; not only weather-wise either.

I swept some files and unpaid bills into a top drawer of my desk, locked it, turned off my computer and, off the hat and coat stand, pulled on my overcoat before reversing the window sign to show CLOSED.

I slammed the self-locking door shut as I ventured into the late afternoon drizzle. As usual, I double-checked my office was actually secure. Looked intently at the engraved brass plate fixed to the black painted door:

**FRANK CONNOR**
PRIVATE ENQUIRIES

Always impressed me: a striking adornment.

Even if my office, formerly an estate agents, wasn't the most impressive building, architecturally speaking, in Hull's Old Town area, with its multi-paned window adjacent to the door. The painted legend above this window reads LAND OF GREEN GINGER, white lettering on a black background. And it is this peculiar name which is also on the nearby street sign. The origins of the name are unknown, but it may refer to the storage of spices in the vicinity during the Middle Ages.

Who knows?

Thinking about it, instead of the brass plate I should have replaced LAND OF GREEN GINGER with my business name. Because, of late business had not been good.

Wondered how long I could continue as a public eye; not a private detective – he detects misdemeanours. I merely make enquiries and pass on my findings to my client. What he, or she, does with the information is entirely up to them. Not as glamorous as the movies suggest. As for my lifestyle, what can I say: underwhelming!

My local government pension has saved me from bankruptcy.

In my mid forties, ready for a change of scenery, I applied for a vacancy as a local authority investigator in the north of England, where I met a girl from Hull. Prior to meeting Amanda, I had never ventured further north than Birmingham. So was pleasantly surprised by East Yorkshire, Hull in particular. My love for a pace of life slower, and it has to be said, in many cases, more friendlier than my birthplace, drew me in. I hail from somewhere down south, is all I am willing to say.

As for Amanda, five good years. Even though we were both relatively young, we were set in our ways. And after the break-up, I never considered returning south.

They say, reaching the half-century mark age-wise is life defining. I was given an opportunity to take an 'early retirement' deal. It wasn't the retirement that interested me, more the monthly pension and lump sum payment that came with it. This enabled me to be my own boss.

A work ethic had been instilled into my psyche by my Irish Protestant parents.

Solicitors in Hull were willing to employ me on an

"as and when" basis: serving legal notices and papers, carrying out pre-trial enquiries.

Hull's legal profession was largely entrenched in the Old Town, an area I have always enjoyed wandering around. In particular, Bowlalley Lane, High Street, Scale Lane, as well as the Land of Green Ginger. The cobbled streets laid hundreds of years ago still hold a fascination for me. And, virtually a stone's throw away from my office, is the very essence of the Old Town: Ye Olde White Harte public house.

To me, socialising is more important than getting blathered. It made sense to live in the area close to my business. When a two bed, first floor apartment became available to rent, I snapped it up.

Seemed an age ago when I watched the signwriter emblazoning my name and new profession on the brass plate. Initially business was good, even though many, especially high ranking police officers, were sceptical of a rookie private enquiry agent's prospects, as well as fearful of me interfering in matters concerning the police.

I received an early call from Detective Inspector Harry Millbank, obviously wanting to discourage me in my new line of work and find an alternative. Fortunately for me, I was able to give him valuable information on a case he was involved with. Consequently, when he was able to, without annoying his superiors, we had, and still have as far as I am aware, a 'you scratch my back' arrangement.

Coincidentally, we discovered we had similar drinking preferences, Ye Olde White Harte being our 'local'.

Strange, because neither of us were local to the area, me being a southerner, Harry a Welshman.

After our first, somewhat acrimonious meeting in my office, he left with a warning, "You want to mind how you go, boyo."

Even now, after four years, DI Millbank can go 'off on one'.

I know I'm in his black book if he addresses me as "Connor".

Recently, on my way to the White Harte for an early evening half of bitter, I caught a glimpse of my reflection in an estate agent's window. I grimaced: the bloke looking back at me appeared shorter than my five-ten, with care worn features. Call me vain, but my concern at this sight led me to the gents' toilet in the pub; had a clearer view of yours truly in the mirror, despite a diagonal crack fracturing the surface. My fairish hair had survived the ravages of time, barring some greying of my sideburns and I suppose a lined forehead and 'crows feet' at the sides of my eyes were the norm for a man of my age.

Made my way to the right hand side bar via the empty beer garden.

The pub is a seventeenth century delight and full of history. I paddled across the grey stone floor, leant on the bar, a high shelf full of glasses above my head; dark wood panelling added to the mystique, the only drawback was that a gas fire had long since replaced a roaring coal fire, Still...

The young barmaid, at my request, pulled a half of bitter, which I drank slowly, as I contemplated joining a gym. Or maybe going for early morning runs.

"Fancy the other half?"

Harry joining me.

We retreated to a nearby table, him with a pint, me with the other half.

"What's up with you, boyo? he asked. "Looks like you've lost a twenty and found a quid."

"How do you do it Harry?

"How do I do what?"

"Keep in shape. Relatively youthful."

"Ey. Watch it with the 'relatively'."

"No, seriously. How do you do it?"

Allowed himself a generous gulp of beer before answering. "Well, no offence... But I would imagine I'm younger than you: forty-four come June. How about you, Frank?"

"You're younger than me."

"And that's never going to change, boyo."

Lifted his glass. "Cheers."

In my office early next morning. Sorting through my bills and finances, trying to reconcile them – to the satisfaction of all concerned. Prior to shuffling my papers, the phone rang.

A strange request: an intermittent client, a rather attractive lady in her sixties said she'd pay me handsomely to look after her dog for a few days. Plus, I could stay in her palatial home situated in an expensive suburb west of Hull. In fact, and I quote "Gigi will receive your utmost care and attention."

I've had some strange jobs in my time, but...

I didn't commit. But having reassessed my options, financially speaking... Picked up the phone to let Mrs Butler-Mayfield I would...

The sudden appearance of Albert Farrar encouraged me to terminate my call.

I'd known Albert for some time. Before I became an enquiry agent. A few years older than me, a genial bespectacled chap with not a bad bone in his body, always smartly dressed, favouring a collar and tie. As I did. His contacts within every corner of the Humberside community were numerous. Early on in our friendship I asked what he did for a living: "Legal consultant".

Yet as far as I know, Albert had no office, wasn't listed in the phone book under 'Solicitors'.

But he was, to me at any rate, invariably on the end of his smart phone when I needed him.

"Good morning, Albert. What can I do for you? Or, hopefully, what can you do for me?"

Sitting on the other side of my desk. "That bad, eh?"

I shoved the batch of unpaid bills towards him. Could tell by the look on his face no business was forthcoming.

"If you have no work for me, Albert, then..."

He pulled a colourful card from his inside jacket pocket, handed it to me. I stared at the psychedelic artwork surrounding the number 75.

Albert cut in, "Turn it over."

The reverse side of the card was an invite to Clive Farrar's 75th birthday party at the Kingston Theatre Hotel, March 10th 2018.

"Your brother's seventy-five?"

"That's what it says, Frank."

"You going, Albert?"

"I organised it."

"Oh."

I paused, not wanting to offend Albert, but parties are not my scene – a life-long aversion.

Ever since my father hauled me along to a party held for the eight-year-old son of a mate of his. Because I was the same age, the old man and his mate were under the impression it would be an enjoyable occasion. But I was a withdrawn, shy kid. Not even the glitter-rock music of T-Rex, a favourite of mine at the time, could chill me out.

"I will see you there, Frank," paused, then added, "You don't know Clive socially. And probably no one else. But me and you – two friends together."

Of course I'll go. Can't let Albert down. "I don't have many friends, Albert. But none better than you. I'll be there."

After sharing coffees and general chit-chat, Albert left. And I was left – with no options.

Lifted the phone. My call was answered with a short "Hello."

"Mrs Butler-Mayfield, about your proposition..."

* * *

"You have the free run of the house." That's what Mrs Butler-Mayfield told me before departing for a business trip in Florida for a week, maybe more.

Her guided tour was impressive. I fully intended to make myself comfortable, looked forward to boosting my fitness levels with the indoor swimming pool. Unbelievingly, she had her very own cinema, with a vast array of old films. To me, this was better than the fifty inch telly, which held no interest: depressing news, lying politicians, modern movies. Fully stocked drinks cabinet; though being a moderate imbiber, there would'nt  be much reduction in stock. In any case, If Mrs Butler-Mayfield found out that I'd been drunk in charge of her dog, I'd still be left with unpaid bills.

That brings me to the dog: Gigi, shaggy-haired, mainly white, with hardly discernible brown patches behind her ears. Diminutive in stature.

My first public appearance with Gigi down at the foreshore, close to the Humber Bridge, attracted strange glances from passers-by. After a short, and I do mean short, walk, she refused to budge. When I seated myself on a bench, she jumped up onto my recently laundered trousers. Ended up carrying Gigi to my car. As I said, strange glances. Thankfully, the dog slept after a feed.

Took the opportunity of completing twenty lengths of the pool and after drying off, stretched out on a recliner. Must have dozed off, because when I checked my wristwatch it showed a time of ten past four.

Casually attired, I wandered into the lounge. To say I was startled by a bloke helping himself to a snifter from the drinks cabinet is an understatement.

"Evening, squire," said the tweed-suited gent. Age around mid sixties, ruddy faced, sporting a handlebar moustache. No doubt compensation for thinning hair.

"Who the hell are you?" was all I could manage.

He moved closer to me, causing me to clutch my hands into fists. Just in case.

"I, dear boy, am Richard Mayfield. And whom do I have the pleasure of speaking to?"

Certainly not from Hull, unless he's had elocution lessons.

"Never mind that. How did you get in, because breaking and entering is a..."

He stopped me in my tracks by holding up a key. "Simple, old fruit." He put down his drink, after gulping down half and went on to explain he was separated from Mrs Butler-Mayfield. Still on friendly terms though. Pops in now and again to see how she is.

Polished off his drink. "Well, must be off. Nice to meet one of Hilary's chums. Toodle-oo."

Now I don't know if I'm becoming daft in middle age. Or Mayfield had hypnotised me.

But after unjumbling my thoughts, I realised he never asked me who I was. Or what I was doing in Mrs B-M's house. And why didn't the bloody dog bark?

DOG?

I hurried through to the utility room, dismayed to see an empty basket.

Didn't take me long to conduct a search of the house. And garden.

No doubt about it though. Gigi had disappeared.

It had been a dark, dingy day and light was beginning to fade as I started the engine of my aging, bottle-green

Ford Escort.

Usually, I like music on car journeys: Miles Davis, Chet Baker, Thelonius Monk. But the quest to find Gigi warranted my full attention. Surely, with her white coat she'd be easy to spot. Forty minutes of travelling through affluent suburbs – and nothing. Gave it another quarter of an hour and returned to base – dogless.

Looked with foreboding at Gigi's empty basket. Could only think, that when Mayfield entered the house, the dog had whipped past him.

Then remembered Mrs B-M had said she would Skype me six-thirty UK time. Checked my watch: not long to go. Bound to want sight of Gigi.

I sank into a comfortable armchair in the lounge. Must've dozed off. Brought back to reality by my smartphone's ringtone. Glanced at the phone resting on the arm of the chair: true to her word, it was Mrs B-M.

Decided to ignore her, hoping Gigi would reappear before her mistress's next inevitable call.

Unfortunately, the next call arrived sooner than I hoped. Probable that Mrs B-M had twigged something was up. Held my phone in front of me, activated Skype.

She looked concerned.

"Hello, Frank. Everything okay?"

She sounded concerned.

I hesitated before responding, "Had a visitor earlier."

"A visitor?"

"Your husband. At least that's what he said."

"Describe him for me."

I described Richard Mayfield. Mrs B-M looked annoyed.

"Why did you let him in?"

"I didn't. He has a key to your house."

"Damned impertinence."

"Gave me the impression you and him are still friendly. Despite being separated."

"That simply is not true, Frank."

I told my employer I was in the pool area when he apparently let himself into her house.

This alarmed Mrs B-M no end. Asked me to check all interior walls for evidence of picture removals. She'd built up an expensive collection and her ex was currently financially embarrassed.

"You think he might've nicked one," I said.

"Not just one."

Carrying my phone, I checked the house for signs of art theft. There were none. No tell-tale residual square or oblong shapes on any of the walls.

"That's a relief," sighed Mrs B-M.

A silence between us. Then she asked me to contact a local locksmith early the following morning and have him change all locks to her property, plus the garage door fastenings.

She then bid me goodnight.

I mimicked her earlier comment – "That's a relief."

Went over to the drinks cabinet, poured myself a small pale ale and returned to my comfy armchair. My relief soon changed to concern: Gigi was still missing.

Mrs B-M must have been reading my thoughts: here she was on Skype once more.

"I forgot to ask how Gigi is, Frank."

Then, before I could respond... "Let's have a look at her. I've missed her."

Carried my phone into the utility room, showed Mrs B-M the empty basket.

"Where is she, Frank?"

No way I could sugar coat this. "Think she must've slipped out when your ex came in.

She'll probably..."

"She never goes out of her own accord. Never."

Thought this job would be a piece of cake, easy money. Well, I can kiss goodbye to my fee on this one.

My phone dispiritedly fell to my side.

"Are you still there Frank? Frank?"

Held up my phone. "Still here."

"It wasn't art Richard wanted. It was Gigi. He's taken her. I'm sure of it," Mrs B-M said worriedly.

"To get back at you?"

"No. Well, yes, partly. He'll sell Gigi. A lot easier. And less suspicious than offloading pictures."

"Gigi's got value?

"You bet." She paused. "You can still have your fee, Frank. But you'll have to earn it."

Knew what was coming. Had to recover her dog.

Armed with Richard Mayfield's address, I exited the house, after setting the alarm, and headed for his home in my Escort, woolly hat on to combat the cold.

A few miles from his ex-marital home, Mayfield's bungalow sat in an elevated position, offering extensive views of the Humber Bridge, the murky, moonlit river rushing below.

Parked around fifty yards away from the detached property. No one around as I approached, listening all the time for Gigi's distinctive bark.

Soon reached Mayfield's abode: subdued lighting in the lounge and, fortunately, no curtains or blinds, making it easy for a nosey. Cursed under my breath as I tripped on the wonky footpath.

Carefully peered through the large picture window: Mayfield stretched out on a three-seater settee watching the news on a large television. No sign of Gigi.

Moved to the side of the bungalow and was confronted by a two metre high gate. Figured Gigi was in the rear garden; me rattling the gate would cause her to bark.

Retreated into the roadway. Too risky to move my car closer; Mayfield will have clocked it on his visit to his ex. And loitering within sight of the bungalow, in the open, on bitterly cold February night didn't appeal. But what choice did I have?

The next hour passed very slowly, with neither sight, nor sound of Gigi. Became paranoid about the possibility of her being sedated by Mayfield.

Several minutes later, he left his bungalow via the front door. I dodged behind a large shrub, peering through the foliage: Richard Mayfield appeared edgy as he ambled over to his garage, looking from right to left intermittently. He unlocked the up-and-over door. Out dashed what appeared to be Gigi. It was one of those occasions when I wished I had the ability to whistle two finger style through my teeth.

The dog's abductor grabbed hold of her by the collar.

Now or never: with my hat pulled down over my face as far as possible to avoid detection, I ran as fast as I could towards man and dog, wrestling the animal from Mayfield and legged it quickly to my motor, where I bungled her onto the rear seat.

Back at my temporary home, Gigi seemed restless, distressed even. Wouldn't stay in her basket.

I Skyped Mrs B-M, who was delighted when I broke the good news.

"Let me see her, Frank."

It was a struggle, but managed to hold the dog for her owner to see.

"Frank, is this some kind of joke?"

Didn't understand. "Pardon?"

"You're not holding Gigi."

Still didn't understand.

"Looks like Gigi, I have to say. Take a closer look, Frank."

I did. "No brown patches."

"Precisely."

Hard to tell whether she said this through clenched teeth.

"You never told me Richard had a dog."

"Well, you know now. Back to the drawing board, Frank."

With that, she was gone. That's the problem with my job – you never get to know the full story. Might be back to the drawing board. But not tonight.

Mounted the stairs after leaving a calmed dog in the utility room. Opened the guest bedroom door: at least a King-size bed greeted me.

Mrs Butler-Mayfield had preset the alarm clock for six-thirty am. No doubt so Gigi could have her early morning walk. Drew back the curtains: wind and sleet.

Wonderful!

A slice of buttered toast and a small cup of coffee was all I could face for breakfast. Living in salubrious surroundings wasn't all it was cracked up to be. Jumped into my Escort and drove close to Mayfield's home, where I let his dog out of my car. Watched Mayfield drag his barking pet inside and drove in the direction of the Old Town.

No sooner had I sat at my desk when the office door opened: Detective Inspector Millbank.

He sat opposite me, a smirk on his face. "Who's been a naughty private enquiry agent?"

So Richard Mayfield recognised me last night.

Bugger!

With relish, Millbank continued, "I'm a bit rusty with dog-napping. Have to check up on one of my law books later. Don't think the legislation's been amended since… oh... 1745. But I feel sure the minimum sentence is..."

"All right, Harry. All right."

"This is official business, boyo. Detective Inspector, to you, Connor."

"You're kidding me. Right?"

He laughed. "Should've warned you about Hilary

Butler-Mayfield, Frank."

"Oh, it's Frank now is it?"

"C'mon. Where's your sense of humour?"

I paused for thought. "What do you mean – you should've warned me?"

"She has an eye for the younger gent. Mind you, you're not far off her age."

"How old is she?"

"Sixty-five. Not a bad-looker for her age, you have to admit."

"Well, I'm nowhere near sixty-five. As well you know. Anyway, she employed me to look after her dog."

"Softening you up, boyo."

"Strictly business as far as I'm concerned."

"Thought your business was private enquiries."

"Yes, well, sometimes, if needs must."

"I see. Business not so good then?"

"Temporarily."

He looked directly at me. "Why? Why did you snatch Mayfield's dog?"

I stood, moved over to the kettle. "Fancy a cup of coffee?"

Over coffee I gave Harry a full explanation.

Plus, I asked for advice on how I could trace Hilary Butler-Mayfield's dog. Had to find Gigi: my livelihood depended on it.

As I was in my office, spent my time sorting out paperwork and filing. In between drinking coffee and wondering where the bloody dog was.

My day ended. Might as well spend the night at Mrs B-M's place, in the hope that, if Gigi had wandered off and become lost, she would find her way back home.

A restless night followed.

I was right off my food, so another meagre breakfast.

After driving around the suburbs and villages, I

headed for the Humber Bridge foreshore at Hessle, where I parked up, took in the ever increasing gloom gathering over the river, wondering if I'd ever lay eyes on Gigi again.

I'm not one for drinking and driving, but a small snifter to lift the gloom: what harm could it do?

The only harm it did was to my wallet. The recently renovated hotel I patronised obviously had to recoup the cost of my plush surroundings. I pushed a ten-pound note towards the barman.

"Keep the change."

"There isn't any," he responded.

"Keep it anyway."

My overpriced drink didn't lift the gloom. It wasn't only the missing Gigi. Doubt if she'll ever grace these parts again. It was my ever-decreasing income.

As Charles Dickens character, Mr Micawber put it: "Annual income twenty pounds, annual expenditure twenty pounds and sixpence. Result misery."

The barman asked if I wanted another drink. Was tempted to reply, "At your prices?"

Instead, I gave him my best hard-boiled detective stare and left. Headed for my car. Switched on the radio. And would you know it, Vic Damone was singing his rendition of GIGI:

*Gigi, am I a fool without a mind.*
*Or have I merely been too blind to realise?*

But like it or not, that dog was presently the only solution to my financial difficulties. With no surplus funds to pay for assistance, I undertook the job of tailing Richard Mayfield on my own. But after five days was no nearer to locating Gigi.

Tired, unshaven and thoroughly cheesed off, I gave the office a miss and returned home, where I quickly undressed and fell into bed at, for me, the early time of nine pm.

Within a minute my phone shrilled for a text: odds on it would be Hilary. Put my phone on 'silent' without checking the screen and closed my eyes.

Woke up around seven. Showered in hot, then tepid water to freshen myself up. After dressing I ate a light breakfast of coffee and buttered toast.

As I moved through to the bedroom to retrieve my phone I remembered last night's text. To my surprise the message was from Albert: just a reminder, Frank – party this coming Saturday. C u there.

This coming Saturday was tomorrow. Needed a party like a hole in the head. Phoned Millbank and arranged to meet him at Ye Olde White Harte, lunch time.

Felt like a brisk walk was in order.

Didn't take me long to reach the old ferry terminal overlooking the River Humber.

Leaning on the railings I glanced to the impressive grey/blue ship-like structure known as The Deep, an aquarium which never failed to stir me on visits.

Then turned my attention to the fast flowing river, hoping for inspiration.

Didn't materialise. Why should it?

Minutes later, passers-by were looking at me – strangely.

Realised I was talking to myself. About Gigi.

Took a vow of silence.

My return walk was not as brisk. More of a stroll. Not concentrating. Because suddenly I found myself alongside the RBS, the infamous bank.

An eastern European voice: "Good morning, Frank."

Looked down: Marek, kept warm by his two border collies – Spick and Span.

Marek, a thirty-something, Polish immigrant down on his luck. Probably five or six quid in his Cafe Nero coffee cup, all in loose change. I added a fiver to it.

Spick seemed to nod in appreciation. I patted his head, tickled him under his chin.

I paused.

"Of course."

"Of course what, Frank?"

"Your dogs. Where did you get your dogs, Marek?"

Hesitation. Knew I was on the right track.

"Marek. You won't be in trouble. I promise."

He pulled his notebook from his inside coat pocket, scribbled on a page, ripped it from the book and handed it to me. Marek was the eyes and ears of the Land of Green Ginger and survived on cash handouts from various police officers and me. A dangerous game, which had resulted in a couple of beatings.

The Pole's note contained the name DIMITROV, residing in a village on the Withernsea road and ended with a request to destroy this information.

Tucked the note into my trousers pocket and contacted Mrs B-M via Skype, appealing for a picture of Gigi to show Marek.

On viewing the dog's photo, he hesitated before shaking his head.

The tell-tale hesitation once more.

Mrs Butler-Mayfield became over-enthusiastic at the thought of being reunited with her beloved dog. I was becoming over-enthusiastic at the thought of being re-united with money.

We negotiated a generous fee, which included a reward (undisclosed to her) for Marek.

Then the veiled threat from my wealthy client: "Don't let me down, Frank."

If Gigi is still with Dimitrov, retrieving her on my own will prove tricky. To say the least.

That is why, in my fee, I included an inducement, if required, for Detective Inspector Millbank, whose assistance, and that of some of his officers, will be necessary to aid my endeavours. In the event of the whole operation going pear shaped, Frank Connor would be seeking pastures new, employment wise.

My scheduled lunchtime meet at Ye Olde White Harte now took on a whole new meaning.

Needless to say, Harry was only too willing to help; no inducement necessary. Because, if successful, bringing down an illegal dog dealer would enhance Millbank's promotion prospects. Quite fancied himself as Detective Chief Inspector.

After ordering halves of bitter, he beckoned me to follow him into the bitterly cold beer garden.

"This is official police business now, boyo."

"Oh yes," I said, knowing what was coming next.

"Yes. Your information may be useful, but… where did you say it came from?"

"I didn't."

Millbank eyed me warily. "Hope you're not becoming involved in something beyond your capabilities, Frank."

Looked the Detective Inspector straight in the face. "Don't bother to thank me. I'm just a concerned citizen doing his public duty."

A smile followed by a half laugh from Millbank. "Hardly."

"What's that supposed to mean?"

"Would imagine Hilary Butler-Mayfield's fee for the return of her dog took priority over your concerned citizenship."

Returned to my beer and casually responded. "You have a way of starting conversation which ends conversation."

A period of silence as we finished our drinks.

Harry clasped my shoulder. "I'll keep you informed."

He left. Lost in my thoughts, I never heard the

barmaid ask if I wanted another drink.

Loudly she said, "I said, do you want a refill?"

Shook my head and left.

* * *

I'm not a party person, as I've already said. But felt I couldn't let Albert down. Besides, he's put a fair bit of work my way since setting up on my own.

Dressed in my best blue suit, off the peg from Marks and Spencer. Didn't want to appear too informal, so I donned a navy blue, button- down collared shirt teamed with a psychedelic designed pink and green tie – present from a grateful client. Or was it an ungrateful client?

I strolled to the Kingston Theatre Hotel, via Queen's Gardens.

A cold night. The dark, inky sky littered with stars. Could've been my imagination, but I swear the Little Dog constellation was prominent in the vastness above me.

Less than ten minutes and I stepped inside the hotel basement, my ears battered by The Beatles blasting out A Hard Day's Night:

*It's been a hard day's night*
*And I've been working like a dog*
*It's been a hard day's night*
*I should be sleeping like a log*

Hear, hear to that. Scanned the room for a familiar face. Found none.

The dance floor was heaving with, mostly, senior members of society, behaving like, presumably, their younger selves. Gyrating in weird manoeuvres, which, to my eye, was conduct unbecoming. This strange exhibition continued when the disc jockey played another Beatles number, Roll Over Beethoven:

*I got the rockin' pneumonia*
*I need a shot of rhythm and blues*
*I caught the rollin' arthritis*
*Sittin' down at a rhythm review*

Just about sums up this crowd.

All of a sudden I felt quite conspicuous, being the only person in the room wearing a tie A tap on the shoulder from behind. Turned.

"Hello, Albert."

He looked me up and down. "It's not fancy dress, Frank. I did tell you. Anyway, who are you supposed to be?"

"Thought I'd come as a psychedelic enquiry agent."

He looked at me, bewildered. Albert himself looked quite ridiculous: tight fitting denims teamed with a 'WHO' T shirt. He paused before speaking.

"Anyway, I'll be with you shortly. Mingle." As he moved away, he added, "And take off your tie. It's ludicrous."

I was now the bewildered one. Made my way to the bar, ordered a large iced Coke. Held it up to the bloke standing next to me, who was of similar appearance, looks wise and fashion wise, to Albert.

"Happy birthday, Clive," I said to him.

He seemed puzzled.

"Frank. Frank Connor," I reminded him.

"Oh yes. We have met. Briefly."

He hesitated, obviously scrutinizing my appearance the same way his brother had. But I beat him to the punchline.

"I've come to your party as a psychedelic enquiry agent. Before you ask."

"Oh, I see. It's not a fancy dress party though," he responded in a kind of effeminate way.

You could've fooled me, I thought.

"Nice to have met you," he said before flouncing off.

Propped up the bar, surveyed my surroundings in more detail: entrance opposite me, white clothed tables teamed with chairs, mostly occupied with partygoers and in a corner, a large empty table, most likely reserved for buffet food later on.

The dance floor was filling up, and, like the rest of the venue, around sixty-forty in the favour of males. Among the throng were a sprinkling of younger couples and a handful of kids, probably aged between eight and thirteen.

After twenty minutes or so my ears had been battered by a musical repertoire ranging from David Whitfield's Cara Mia (know what you're thinking: who the hell is David Whitfield?) I'll tell you: a former building labourer from Hull, who had a string of operatic type songs during the 1950s. As I was saying, from Whitfield to David Bowie belting out 'The Jean Genie', an obvious favourite with most people, who joined in with the chorus.

Ventured outside for a breath of fresh air. And peace and quiet. It was times like this I wished I was a smoker. Tried to clear my cluttered mind.

Shrill of my phone. Instinctively, I answered: Mrs Butler-Mayfield.

God, she's impatient. She came right to the point: "Where is Gigi?"

"Getting awful tired of answering that question," was my flat response.

Perked up a bit when she mentioned a bonus on a quick return of her pet. After thanking her she ended the call.

"Thought you'd be inside. In the warm. Enjoying the party," - Albert's unwanted comments. But couldn't afford to be on the wrong side of him.

I endured a further hour of musical punishment;

suppose it was too much to ask, which I did, of the DJ to chuck in some Miles Davis' trumpet classics. The DJ had never heard of Miles Davis. Ray Davies of The Kinks, yes. But not Miles.

At one point I had to tolerate a happy-clappy disco song, requested by a group of youngsters, who formed a circle on the dance floor and performed a 'hands above heads' routine to said song. One of the dancers, a forty-something, heavily made-up, blonde woman beckoned a shy young boy to join her. When he shook his head in refusal, she attempted to drag him into the circle, to no avail. And much to her annoyance.

I'd spotted the lad earlier. He was quite content in his own company, tapping away on his smartphone. Presumably the blonde was his mother. I felt for the kid.

Still, wouldn't be thanked for butting in. Made my way to the Gents. Guy next to me peed on my shoes. Thankfully, the geezer to my left was experiencing difficulty in urinating.

"Great party," he said.

"Yeah. Great party," I said indifferently.

Before he continued with what I knew he would continue with, I put him straight. "I've come as a private enquiry agent."

That shut him up.

As I zipped up, I heard ferocious vomiting from inside one of the cubicles. That does it, I thought. I'm out of here.

My exit was blocked by a worried Albert: three, possibly four old dears had been robbed of their handbags.

"Albert, see this suit? It's the suit of a private enquiry agent. Call the police."

I departed. Determined the night was not going to be a complete waste of time. Within ten minutes I was heading towards the eastern suburbs in my ancient Ford

Escort.

Not much traffic. Reached my destination reasonably quickly. To my dismay, I spotted DI Millbank's motor: a fairly new Audi A4. A few weeks ago he treated me to a spin in his pride and joy.

"Must've cost you a fortune," I said, without the slightest trace of envy.

"I can afford it. Work hard. And this is one of my rewards."

Then a stupid smirk across his face.

"A proper job, like mine, Frank... well, makes for an easier life. Financial security so to speak. Know what I mean, boyo?"

Sometimes his sarcasm got right up my nose. "I'm my own boss though, Harry. Answerable to no one."

"Yes. And look where it's got you," he said while overtaking a slowcoach on a dual carriageway.

I parked well away from Millbank's Audi. From out of my windscreen I could see high razor wire topped fencing protecting the dog farm. Stepped out of my car into a night lit up by the moon. My breath into the cold night air alerted someone with a bright beam torch, which dazzled me.

"What the devil are you doing here?" DI Millbank's gruff Welsh tone.

No time to answer, "Told you. This is police business," he added.

No time either for further conversation as all hell broke loose: flashing blue lights, screeching brakes, uniformed coppers leaping out of blue and yellow checked cars and vans.

Millbank left me to supervise operations. His initial task being to instruct two burly, anti-riot dressed officers to cut off gate padlocks with massive bolt croppers; this set off a cacophony of dog barking.

I let them get on with it and after several minutes

entered the dog compounds. Looking for Gigi. Armed with Hilary Butler-Mayfield's latest photo.

Astonishingly, I wandered around this muddy, disorganised dog dealership without one single copper asking who I was. Never seen so many dogs in one place.All shapes and sizes: pekes, pugs, Alsatians and Airedales, collies and corgis. Hopefully, among this lot is Gigi, a rather cute, expensive scruff. Began calling her name. Had to dodge behind a shed, because I'd alerted Millbank.

Decided to take a different path, periodically calling out "Gigi".

Ten minutes or so of this without success. Despondency setting in.

Via a back path, I traipsed towards my car and came across a middle-aged woman sporting a monogrammed, green fleece. She was bent down and up close I could see the motif DOGHOUSE emblazoned in gold lettering on her fleece. I could also see she was talking and trying to encourage a reluctant dog to do her bidding.

Wasn't sure, but tried anyway, "Gigi. C'mon, girl."

The dog acknowledged me, strained on her leash.

The startled woman stood up, faced me in an intimidating manner, her wrinkled features full of confrontation. Quickly, I flashed my ID, hoping it resembled a police warrant card.

"You're facing criminal charges. This is a stolen dog," I said, with as much authority as I could muster.

"You're not a copper. Been around them long enough to know one when I see one."

Bugger. She's not playing ball. Tried wrestling Gigi, by now highly stressed, away from 'wrinkly features', but failing.

The tussle between us caused Gigi to bark continuously. Heard running behind me. Flashlights lit up our space. Turned to see Harry heading a posse of uniformed police officers.

DI Millbank didn't seem too pleased to see me. Held up my hands in surrender. Unfortunately, this allowed the woman to make a run for it, Gigi tucked under an arm.

Frantically, I pointed at them, "Get her, Harry. She has Gigi."

The Detective Inspector motioned for his men to apprehend the dognapper. Which they duly did. Gigi ran towards me, almost jumping into my beckoning arms. Made a fuss of her. Sure my policeman friend would not be making a fuss of me!

"For you, a happy ending, Connor. But I'll not tolerate you poking your nose into police affairs again. Last warning, boyo."

He requested Gigi's collar and lead for DNA testing, dropping them into an evidence bag.

"Don't know why I'm doing this," he said, writing on the bag label. "Chances of catching the dog's kidnapper are zero". He scowled. "About as much chance as you not sticking your oar in again. Every man and his dog has touched that lead."

Resisted the temptation to say, "Is that a joke?"

Gigi happily accompanied me back to my car. She sat alongside me as I Skyped her owner. Mrs Butler-Mayfield squealed with delight on seeing her beloved Gigi. The dog couldn't understand why there was distance between them.

Cleared my throat nervously. "Fee as agreed, Mrs Butler-Mayfield?"

"Most definitely. More business to come your way I can tell you that. And call me Hilary. Mrs Butler whatsit makes me feel old."

"Will do, Mrs But... Hilary."

"Speak in the morning to arrange picking up Gigi.

Thanks a million, Frank."

And with that, she was gone.

Within forty minutes, a contented private enquiry agent and contented dog, were safe in my apartment. She looked up at me with pleading, chocolate brown eyes.

Don't know why, but I began singing to her: my gentle version of A Hard Day's Night.

*Been a hard day's night*
*And I've been working like a dog*
*Been a hard day's night,*
*I should be sleeping like a log*

On a winner here. Knelt down and continued.

*But when I get home to you*
*I find the things that you do*
*Will make me feel alright*

Gigi began whining. Maybe should try her song: Gigi.

*Gigi, I am a fool without a mind*
*Or have I...*

"My voice that bad, Gigi?  Or am I indeed a fool without a mind?"

She began barking. Either she agrees. Or she's hungry. I fed her. Toddled off into my bedroom and before I had completely undressed, Gigi leapt onto the duvet. Our tiredness caught up with both of us.

Gigi was my alarm call many hours later. After breakfast she walked with me to my office, where she was happy to lounge on an old blanket I'd taken with me. Sitting at my desk, I opened what I had christened my ‘Debt Drawer’ and collected all my bills and invoices together, placed them in priority order and brought up the adding machine App on my phone.

Gigi barked, rushed to the front door. Gingerly, Albert peered into my office.

“Steady, Gigi. It’s only Albert.”

She returned to her basket.

“Didn’t know you had a dog,” said Albert, sitting opposite me.

“I don’t.”

Albert gave me a quizzical look, spreading his hands.

“Dog sitting. For a client. A fee paying client?”

“A fee paying client.”

“Well, you’re not going to make much money that way, Frank” he said, with a chuckle.

“And I’ve not been making much money from referrals from you, Albert. In fact, you’ve not put much work my way at all lately.”

“Not strictly true. Not too late to investigate Clive’s party thefts.”

“Harry’s problem.”

“DI Millbank?”

“Yep. Told me only last night he doesn’t want me poking my nose into police business. I take it the party ended prematurely.”

“For some, yes. But quite a few of us made the best of it. As a matter of fact, the night ended rather well for me.”

“Excuse me?”

Albert pulled something from his inside coat pocket and moved to my side of the desk, his beery breath from last night invading my nostrils. The item taken out of his pocket was a postcard size, colour photograph of a young female brunette, attired in a skimpy, black bathing suit. At least, I think it was a swimsuit.

“What do you think, Frank?”

"Looks familiar."

"Remember the girl behind the bar last night?"

"Ah, yes."

"We got chatting. Had a few things in common actually."

"Really?"

Albert ignored my incredulity. But continued. "She gave me this photo. Think she's too young for me, Frank?"

Eyed him warily. "When she's fifty, you'll be a hundred."

As he snatched the photo off me, the front door opened. Then closed. Noisily. Detective inspector Harry Millbank appeared far from amused. Though his demeanour didn't prevent Albert trying to impress him with the photograph. Millbank swatted it away. Like a troublesome fly.

Then, pointing at me, "I want a word with you, boyo."

He scowled at Albert. "In private."

I motioned for Albert to make himself scarce. This he reluctantly did.

"Fancy a cup of tea?" I enquired of Harry, moving over to the kettle.

He barred my way.

"You were parked close to my car last night."

"Well, wouldn't say close."

He was incensed now. "I've told you before, boyo. Time and time again. To conduct your own affairs. And not interfere..."

Held up my hands in surrender. "I know. Keep away from police business. Which I did. Up to a point. Anyway, what have my parking arrangements got to do with anything?"

"Vigilance. Vigilance is a priority in law enforcement."

"Ah, but I'm not in law enforcement. I'm an enquiry agent."

"Stop splitting hairs, Connor."

"What's this all about, Harry?"

"What's this all about?"

"Yes. I don't know what the hell you're driving at."

Harry paced the floor for several moments. Finally stopped. Looked me straight in the eye.

"Some bugger's nicked my Audi!"